"You won't have to hide anymore, Eloise," Jackson said. "Then it won't be dangerous for either of you."

"You can't promise me that," Eloise said, anger giving her strength. "You promised me that once before, remember? And I almost lost my baby girl. I gave her up to protect her and I won't change on that. I have to stay away from her for the same reason."

His hand on her arm steadied her, but the warmth she felt from his touch only added to her misery. Because she'd put him in danger, too. He'd die for her; she knew that. And she couldn't have that on her conscience.

* * *

PROTECTING THE WITNESSES:

New identities, looming danger and forever love in the Witness Protection Program.

Books by Lenora Worth

Love Inspired Suspense

Fatal Image
Secret Agent Minister
Deadly Texas Rose
A Face in the Shadows
Heart of the Night
Code of Honor
Risky Reunion

Steeple Hill

After the Storm
Echoes of Danger
Once Upon a Christmas
"'Twas the Week
  Before Christmas"

Love Inspired

The Wedding Quilt
Logan's Child
I'll Be Home for Christmas
Wedding at Wildwood
His Brother's Wife
Ben's Bundle of Joy
The Reluctant Hero
One Golden Christmas
When Love Came to Town
Something Beautiful
Lacey's Retreat
Easter Blessings
  "The Lily Field"
**The Carpenter's Wife*
**Heart of Stone*
**A Tender Touch*

Blessed Bouquets
  "The Dream Man"
†*A Certain Hope*
†*A Perfect Love*
†*A Leap of Faith*
Christmas Homecoming
Mountain Sanctuary
Lone Star Secret
Gift of Wonder
The Perfect Gift
Hometown Princess

*In the Garden
**Sunset Island
†Texas Hearts

LENORA WORTH

has written more than forty books, most of those for Steeple Hill. She has worked freelance for a local magazine, where she wrote monthly opinion columns, feature articles and social commentaries. She also wrote for the local paper for five years. Married to her high school sweetheart for thirty-five years, Lenora lives in Louisiana and has two grown children and a cat. She loves to read, take long walks, sit in her garden and go shoe shopping.

LENORA WORTH
RISKY REUNION

Steeple
Hill®

Published by Steeple Hill Books™

Special thanks and acknowledgment
to Lenora Worth for her contribution to the
Protecting the Witnesses miniseries.

STEEPLE HILL BOOKS

**Steeple
Hill®**

Recycling programs
for this product may
not exist in your area.

ISBN-13: 978-0-373-44397-0

RISKY REUNION

Copyright © 2010 by Harlequin Books S.A.

www.SteepleHill.com

Printed in U.S.A.

He reveals the deep things of darkness
and brings deep shadows into the light.
—*Job* 12:22

To Nate
Thank you so much!

ONE

MEMO: Top Secret/Top Priority

TO: FBI Organized Crime Task Force; U.S. Marshal's Office

FROM: Jackson McGraw, Special Agent in Charge, Chicago Field Office

RE: Operation Black Veil

Federal Bureau of Investigation
Date: June 2, 2010

Chicago Mafia kingpin Salvatore Martino is dead. Per informant—Vincent Martino, now the head of the Martino crime family, will make good on a final tribute to his father by executing Eloise Hill, the woman who testified against Salvatore twenty-two years ago.

Recent sightings place Vincent Martino in Montana—READ—he intends to oversee this hit himself. Through joint investigation with the U.S. Marshal's office, we've learned that even though Eloise Hill left the Witness Protection Program, she is still living in Montana under an assumed name. Current location and name—on a "need to know" basis. Agents currently in place. Witness under twenty-four-hour surveillance. Subject will be immediately informed of these developments and will remain under protection until suspect is apprehended.

Please contact SAC Jackson McGraw on any new leads or changes regarding the above information or any new developments in the Martino case.

Special Agent Jackson McGraw did a visual sweep of the trees on the other side of the little stream then watched as a butterfly fluttered around a cluster of vivid pink bitterroot blooming just outside the window of the vacant apartment he'd been holed up in since 3:00 a.m.

The brown, yellow-tipped butterfly was beautiful, a quiet and graceful contrast to the tension coiled like a snake inside Jackson's gut. Something wasn't right.

Something hadn't been right for the past six months, but now he instinctively knew *that something* was about to go all wrong, completely wrong, if he didn't move quickly. This entire investigation had boiled down to one thing—he had to keep Eloise Hill alive.

But in order to do that, he had to find the leak that seemed to stem from the U.S. Marshal's office, a leak that had jeopardized the entire Witness Protection Program and caused a number of people to be killed. And he had to find Vincent Martino and stop him, one way or another.

Jackson thought back on his last conversation with his informant—the Veiled Lady—back in Chicago two weeks ago. They'd met on a sunny day near a heavily wooded park by the lake. But even though the day had verged on being warm, the woman had worn the same outfit she always wore—a wide-brimmed black hat with a heavy veil covering her face and a black wool coat, gloves and dark shades. And there under the cover of trees surrounding the secluded park, she'd told Jackson the very thing he didn't want to hear.

The woman spoke in a whispery, low voice, her words slow and carefully formal. "Salvatore is dead. He died late last night in his home with several of his top capos there by his side. Vincent was there, too, but as soon as his father is buried, he will be leaving for Montana. He is going to find this woman—Eloise Hill—and finish the job himself. This will be his final tribute to his father. As if Salvatore Martino would care one way or another. The man had no heart." She'd paused, taking a deep breath that almost sounded like a sob. "And neither does his son."

Those chilling words spoken two weeks ago contrasted sharply with the beautiful June morning, Jackson thought now as he looked out the window. His gaze didn't stay on the butterfly. He was watching the other apartment just across the quaint little bridge between the chalet-style brown-and-beige buildings. And he was waiting for the woman who lived there to turn on a light, indicating she was up for the day.

Finally, he'd get to see her and make sure she was all right with his own eyes.

This had been a long journey, trying to find Eloise Hill before Vincent Martino did. She called herself Ellie Smith now, but she would always be Eloise—*his* Ellie—to Jackson. He'd often called her Ellie many years ago. And apparently, she would always be a threat to the powerful Martino crime family, since Vincent Martino was determined to see her dead. Jackson had the body count to prove it, and he was determined to end Vincent's obsession with revenge. He had to warn Eloise. He had to protect her.

And he also had to tell her that her daughter, Kristin Perry, knew about Eloise and wanted to see her.

The static in his earpiece broke the taut summer silence of the early morning. "Big Mac, come in."

Frowning at the nickname his team member Roark Canfield used, Jackson answered. "Talk to me."

"Subject is late for work, sir."

"So I noticed. It's not her day off, is it?"

"Negative. She always leaves at sunrise. She walks a short distance to work just after sunup, no matter the exact time, and she has a big dog with her, sir. Really big German shepherd—dangerous animal."

"I get it about the dog, Roark," Jackson said. "GQ, what's the status at your location?"

"She's not here, sir," Marcus Powell answered from his spot at the restaurant around the corner. "Staff arrived right on time and everyone's busy preparing for the day." A pause, then, "But the one named Verdie has tried calling her several times. No answer. Verdie seems a bit worried from the conversation going back and forth behind the counter."

Jackson rubbed a hand down his neck, the tension going from coiled to twisted. "We're sure of this schedule? Thea, what's your take?"

A feminine voice purred across the line. "Her restaurant is a popular spot, and subject is never late for work. Or at least she hasn't been in the time we've been watching her."

"Affirmative," GQ added. "Staff of three comes in around five every morning to prepare for breakfast rush, but proprietor and two part-timers come in later, just in time for the crowd. Subject stays after lunch to prepare next day's menu from what we've seen so far. She should be on her way by now, sir." Silence, then GQ said, "Uh, Jackson, we have another problem, too. One of the coworkers is also late. Young, blonde, pretty. Her name tag says Meredith. She's usually at the door before anyone else."

Jackson looked at his watch. It was six-fifteen on a Tuesday morning. The sun had been up a good twenty minutes and was now brightening the morning sky with each ticking second. And his gut was burning as hot as those incoming rays. Had the bad gone to worse already?

"I'm on it," he said, his mind ticking off all the logical explanations while his stomach sizzled with the worst-case scenario. "Cover me."

"You got it," Roark said.

Jackson checked his holster, secured his weapon, did a quick surveillance of the nearby city park and the walking trail between buildings, then opened the front door a crack. With Roark stationed in the park and Thea in a car down the way, he didn't need to worry about being secure. But he sure wasn't prepared to see Eloise just yet.

He hadn't planned on announcing himself this abruptly, but Eloise might already be in trouble.

Glancing around, he stalked along the perimeter of the trees, his heart pounding a heavy beat that matched the thud of his hiking boots against gravel. He hit the footbridge over the stream with a run, the echo of his steps chasing him with an eerie cadence across the arched structure.

He was about to come face-to-face with the woman he'd loved for over twenty years. And he prayed he'd find her alive.

She couldn't stop shaking. First the roses and now this. Eloise stared at the clock on the wall of her kitchen, a forgotten cup of coffee steaming in her hand. She had to steady herself to keep from spilling the coffee. Her German shepherd, Duff, rubbed his nose against her robe, trying to get her attention. Duff could sense her trauma and her fear.

Touching a hand to the faithful dog, Eloise gently pushed him away then glanced at the trash can where she'd tossed the white roses. White with pink-edged petals.

Duff sniffed and whined, giving her some measure of comfort. She should have taken him with her last night when she'd deliberately gone out the door to help her friend, but she'd been afraid Duff's barks would bring too much attention to the situation. She'd promised Meredith no cops, but Eloise wished she hadn't kept that promise. She'd arrived only to find her friend dead.

This can't be happening again, she thought, her stomach roiling as a wave of nausea assaulted her. Memories from two decades ago, brutal and raw, hit her with the force of a fist in her solar plexus. She could still see the blood everywhere, could still see Danny's face as he'd begged for his life there in the seedy warehouse in South Chicago. Could still see the quick burst of smoke from the guns and hear the staccato spew of the silencers—once, twice—as Danny and another man were killed in cold blood while she watched from the shadows.

Killed in cold blood. Twenty-two years of trying to forget and it all still seemed as if it had happened last night. Twenty-two years of hiding, of staying invisible, of living like a shadow, always looking over her shoulder. And always wondering what had happened to the child she'd been forced to leave behind. She'd found solace in her faith, in her church and in her work.

She'd almost found a sense of peace.

And now, she'd witnessed another murder.

Remembering the elaborate spray of white roses at Danny's funeral, Eloise rubbed a finger over the scar near her lips. Back then, the Martino family had sent the roses. Salvatore Martino loved roses; he grew them in the massive garden inside the Martino compound.

And he sometimes sent them to the funerals of his victims.

She'd received a box of her own yesterday just before closing at the café. A dozen long-stemmed, lush roses—a creamy white with just the blush of pink around the tips of the petals.

And no card.

She'd been so paranoid she'd rushed out of the café, hurrying down the street with Duff right on her heels and the box of roses still crushed in her arms.

Who sent them? Who knew she was here?

Putting the horrible questions out of her mind, Eloise sank down in a chair, her thoughts reeling with what she'd seen and heard last night after she'd arrived at Meredith's. Screams, a scuffle, then a distinctive thump and footsteps running, running. A man's voice crying out, "No, no." Then Meredith. Dead. Sweet, innocent Meredith. Her friend and her employee. Dead. Lying in a deserted parking lot, blood pooling underneath her head, her eyes open and vacant as she stared up into the night sky.

It seemed as if Meredith had been staring right up at Eloise, asking her why she hadn't come sooner.

"Come up the back stairs," Meredith had shouted over the phone. "He's in the kitchen. I think he knows, Ellie. He's going to kill me. Hurry! You have to get me out of here."

"I'll be there and I'll call 911."

"No!" Meredith was adamant. "No cops. They won't help me. They won't—they'll side with him. Just hurry!"

"Why didn't I get there in time, Lord?" Eloise whispered in a prayer for forgiveness. She shivered in spite of the summer morning and Duff's efforts to console her. She'd tried to help her friend and she'd failed.

Meredith called her, crying and frantic, in the middle of the night. Eloise rushed into the dark night, her own fears somehow pushed aside in order to get Meredith away from her abusive husband. But she'd arrived too late.

"Why didn't I get there sooner? Why didn't I call 911 to help you?" She reached for Duff, rubbing her hand over his soft brown fur. "Why didn't I take you with me, boy?"

But Eloise knew the answer to all of those questions. The roses. She'd been so afraid to leave her house after she'd received the roses. She didn't even take her car. She'd walked the few blocks to Meredith's house. And now, she had to stay hidden, had to stay out of the limelight. She couldn't risk the glare of cameras and reporters and questions from the local authorities. Because she couldn't trust anyone to help her, either. Not even the police.

If she'd been able to step forward sooner, to alert the authorities that Meredith's husband was dangerous, their plan might have worked. Meredith would have gone to a safe place. But Meredith didn't want to go to the local authorities, Eloise reminded herself now. Meredith knew, just as Eloise did, that sometimes the police were actually part of the problem. So they agreed to keep quiet and Eloise finally talked Meredith into escaping. They formed a solid plan, talked about it quietly and secretly for weeks. Everything was in place. And Meredith was finally ready to leave.

But apparently, Meredith's husband had figured things out.

And for that reason, her friend was now dead.

And she was paralyzed with a fear she'd been running from for over twenty years. Paralyzed because Meredith's husband had still been there at Meredith's house last night when she arrived. He stood over the still body, crying quietly as he stared down at his dead wife. A killer crying in regret over the woman he'd murdered.

And that killer might have seen Eloise.

It was just a glimpse in the dark, she reminded herself. He couldn't have caught a good look at her. And since she'd disguised herself with a big hat and a scarf, she prayed he couldn't identify her. But he'd heard her intake of breath, heard the shocked gasp as she stood on the landing above, her silhouette hidden in the shadows.

But he hadn't come after her. Yet.

No one had come after her. Yet.

But the roses…the roses meant that Randall Parker might not be the only person who wanted her dead and gone.

Had the Mob found her after all these years?

"I have to get to work," she said, forcing herself out of the chair, her knuckles white from clutching her now-cold coffee. "I have to pretend everything is all right."

Putting her cup in the sink, Eloise glanced at the

clock. She was late and she was never late. Verdie had already called once, concerned. Verdie would send Frank to look for her.

Meredith won't be there this morning, either.

Meredith would never be at work again.

Her limbs stiff and fatigued from tension and lack of sleep, Eloise managed to get dressed and pull herself together, doing her usual routine of downplaying her looks by pulling her hair away from her face and putting on brown contacts and dowdy clothes. No makeup, but then she rarely wore any—except for a bit of concealer over her scar. She tried to make herself plain and unre-markable and she prayed that ploy would work today. She had to act normal, as if nothing had happened. She had to go through the motions. She knew how to go through the motions; she'd been doing that for so long now it was like second nature.

She'd made it to the hallway, Duff right by her side, when a knock at the front door caused her to drop her purse. It thumped against the tile floor, making her flinch with fear and causing Duff to go wild, barking angrily as he sensed her tension and fear. Picking the purse up again, Eloise slipped her hand into the hidden side compartment where she kept her pistol.

"Duff, sit," she said, trying to sound firm. The big dog whimpered, barked once more, then did as she commanded. But his snarl and his quivering body indi-cated he would attack if she gave him the word.

Shaking, Eloise adjusted the small gun in her hand, its familiar steel giving her a sense of reassurance.

But her mind whirled between running out the back door and remembering the gun-training courses she'd taken.

Lord, help me, she prayed. *I'm so very tired of running. I'm so very tired of being afraid.*

Eloise took a deep breath, gave Duff another command to stay, then walked toward the front door. "Who is it?" she called, her voice weak underneath the heavy, throbbing pulse pumping through her ears.

No reply. She swallowed, once, twice, pulling the gun out of her bag. Then she forced herself to look through the peephole. A man she didn't recognize stood at her door. "I said who's there?" But something about this man—

"It's me," came the terse answer. "It's me…Jackson McGraw. Eloise, open the door and let me in, please."

Jackson stood back, gun at the ready, as the door creaked open about an inch. He turned, doing a quick scan of the surrounding area. Roark jogged by, looking laid-back and casual in spite of the intensity of the situation. Satisfied that his team was still in place, Jackson slowly turned back to the door and put his gun away. Flashing his badge and ID, he said, "It's Jackson. I have to talk to you."

He heard an intake of breath then the door swung back.

And he took in the sight of her, standing there, her eyes wide with shock and fear, her skin pale as she tried to find air. Jackson heard the dog's snarl but ignored it.

"Eloise," he said, reaching for the door.

She swayed, her eyes fluttering, her head dropping.

Jackson stepped inside and caught her before she passed out. The dog went into a frenzied stance, barking and dancing in circles. Jackson issued a sharp command. The animal kept snarling but he stayed away.

"Eloise, it's all right. It's going to be all right."

She felt tiny in his arms, fragile. She looked almost the same, older but still beautiful in spite of the jagged white scar bursting through the pale skin near her lips and the deep circles of fatigue underneath her eyes. And she was still afraid. Her whole body began to quiver with a gentle shaking as she held on to him, her head moving in denial against his shoulder.

"Subject safe," he said. "Stand down." He clicked off his wire with a touch to his wrist, shutting down any further communications for the sake of privacy.

Slamming the door with a booted kick, he helped her to the floral couch then carefully sat her down against the cushions, grabbing a blue chenille blanket off the back. After making sure she was coherent and her dog wasn't going to eat him alive, he sat down beside her. And looked into her eyes again. They were brown instead of the vivid green he remembered, but the colored contacts matched the rich brown of her long, straight hair. Contacts might change the color of her eyes but he didn't care. That look of fear mixed with disbelief and a bit of wonder broke Jackson's heart and made him even more determined to protect her.

"Are you okay?" he asked. "Want some water?"

She shook her head, focusing on him. "What are you doing here?"

The whispered question hung in the air between them. He tried to formulate an answer. But before he could, she sat straight up, asking the same question again, this time with more strength and a defiant demand, realization clearing her eyes. "Why are you here, Jackson?"

Jackson took her hand then inhaled a deep breath. He'd always been straight with her before. He had to tell her the truth now. "Salvatore Martino has died and his son Vincent is here in Montana. And he's looking for you. He's put out a hit on you as a final tribute to the old don."

She pulled away, her mind filling with a dark dread. Wrapping her arms across her midsection, she started rocking back and forth, a low moan escaping between her tightly clenched lips. "No, no, that can't be. Tell me this isn't happening! Not now, not now." She waved a hand in the air, pointing toward the kitchen. "The roses. I got roses yesterday, Jackson. White roses. In the trash."

Jackson glanced toward the kitchen then fell on one knee in front of her, his hands stilling her movements as he held her by the shoulders and forced her to look at him. "It's the truth and that's why I'm here. I'm going to protect you, Eloise. We'll find him before he finds you, I promise." Needing her to listen, he asked, "Who sent you roses? What are you talking about?"

She looked up at him, her eyes widening, her body going still. Jackson was afraid she was going into shock.

"Eloise?"

And then she did something that scared him even more than the fear and shock in her eyes.

She burst out laughing.

TWO

Eloise pushed away the glass Jackson offered her, slapping at his hand. Water sloshed out and fell in a bright pool onto the wooden floor. Duff, now calm, immediately lapped at the water. Jackson set the glass on the table, wiped his hand on his jeans then stared down at her. "Eloise?"

Eloise realized her laughter had turned to tears and that Jackson was staring at her, the frown on his face an indicator of how much she'd confused and frightened him. She'd managed to frighten the fearless Jackson McGraw. That was a first. Or at least she remembered him as fearless, even at age twenty-three and even though he'd been a rookie back then. But he still looked that way—fearless, intense, completely serious and devoted to his job. Only now, he also looked self-confident and sure and a bit weary. His eyes were still that crystal-blue that reminded her of a deep, still lake, but his hair, once a golden brown, now held hints of glinting gray. It suited him.

Her fearless protector. And the man she'd trusted with her most precious possession—her child.

"I'm all right," she said, wiping at her eyes. She

didn't have the luxury of falling apart. She'd never had that luxury. "You just…surprised me." She waved a hand at him. "I saw the irony of my situation and it… seemed so funny. But we both know it's not so funny, is it?"

"Not that I can see, no," he replied, his eyes scanning her, obviously looking for signs of delusional behavior. "You were late for work. I was worried."

"How'd you know— You've been spying on me?"

He nodded. "I'll explain." Then he turned to stare straight into her eyes, his look telling her more than the official report ever could. He was here for a reason; that was how Jackson operated. No need to read more into that intimate look. No need to hope for anything more.

"I'm sure you will."

From habit, she moved a hand down the right side of her face. Had he noticed the scar she'd tried to cover each and every day since the last time he'd seen her? She didn't care about *how* it looked—but the *why* bothered her—the jagged, circular imprint left from the near-death of Eloise and her baby always reminded her of a rose just about to bud.

And roses only reminded her of Salvatore Martino.

"I knew they were coming," she said. "Someone sent me roses yesterday. They were delivered at the café."

"And you think they're from the Martino family?"

She nodded. "Remember how he loved roses?"

Jackson grunted. "He liked to send them to his enemies, just as a polite way of reminding them who was in charge."

"Yes, and he also sent them to funerals, Jackson. There was a big spray at Danny's funeral. I saw them when you took me there before the mourners came in. But I never said anything about them."

He sat back on his heels. "And the roses you got yesterday look like those?"

"Yes. Kind of ironic, don't you think—that my scar looks like a budding rose. Salvatore never knew it, but he left his mark on me." She turned her head, showing the scar to Jackson. "White with traces of pink. It didn't heal very well."

Chilling, considering Salvatore had no qualms about murdering people and letting them bleed, their blood as bright as any *red* roses she'd ever seen.

Jackson's gaze followed her hand as she rubbed it over the scar.

"You're still beautiful," he said, the words so soft she almost missed them. But she couldn't miss the way his gaze settled on her with a protective warmth. "Listen, I'll check on the roses—find out where they came from, okay? Are you sure you're all right?"

She bobbed her head. "Just peachy. And how about you?" She remembered reading his identification and his badge. "Special Agent in Charge now, huh? You've come a long way."

He shrugged. "Yeah, but I've still got a long way to go. And a lot to talk about with you."

She didn't tell him that she'd often thought of him knocking at her door, that she'd dreamed of a moment such as this where they'd be free and clear and together again. She didn't dare tell him any of that. But in her dreams, she hadn't imagined a madman tracking her down at the same time she'd just witnessed another man killing his wife. What were the odds? Hysterical laughter bubbled in her throat again but Eloise forced it back down. It became like bile sitting cold in her stomach.

Willing herself to stay still, she looked back up at him. "What do I do now?"

He looked at his watch. "You should have been at work an hour ago." Before she could respond, he pushed at a tiny wireless earpiece in his left ear, then clicked at his wrist. "GQ, Roark, you read?"

Apparently GQ and Roark did read. Jackson lifted an eyebrow then spoke into thin air. "Subject has been apprised of situation. Stay put. Watch my back. Thea, go back to the command post. I'll update when we meet back up." Satisfied, he looked back at her then turned off the two-way communications device.

"You brought a posse?" she asked, calmer now in spite of the tiny shivers that refused to leave her body.

He nodded, glanced at Duff. "And you bought a dog."

"He's my second one. Do you blame me?"

Jackson didn't answer right away. Instead, he stalked around the confines of her tiny living room like a giant cat, his nostrils lifting, his eyes scanning her minimalist existence with a laserlike scrutiny, his expression blank and unreadable. Reaching out a hand toward Duff, he let the big dog sniff his knuckles. "What's upstairs?"

"A bedroom and a bath," she replied, amazed that her highly trained guard dog seemed to accept Jackson as an immediate ally. But then, Jackson was that way—quiet and calm, and capable, offering a solid security to anyone who needed his help. "Half bath down here and a small laundry and storage room off the back. Two entries—the front door here and the back door off the laundry room. Dead bolts and chain locks on both. And I have a security system and an upstairs exit route. I know the rules, Jackson. And you still haven't answered my questions."

He pushed at his thick, spiked hair, a long sigh his only answer for now. After a minute of looking the place over again, he said, "First, we need to move you."

"I don't want to be moved," Eloise responded, digging in her heels even as the words came out. "I'm settled here and as you apparently already know, I have a good job."

"Risky, opening your own business."

"I took the risk. I set it up under a corporate name and I was very careful with all the paperwork. I needed something to focus on. And baking is the one thing that brings me a sense of peace and normalcy."

The unspoken things hung like high clouds there in the air between them. But Eloise knew he was thinking the same thing she was. Finally, because she knew she might not get a straight answer from him on anything unless he decided she needed to hear it, she dared to ask one more question.

"Jackson, I need to know. Just tell me…is she safe? Is she okay? Is my daughter okay?"

Jackson turned to face her, his hands on his hips, his frigid eyes turning a liquid blue. "She is now."

Eloise's brief joy turned to a familiar dread but that dread brought her courage back. "What do you mean— she is now? And stop evading me, Jackson. You came to me. And if you want to protect me, you'd better level with me. I need the truth—not just the 'need to know.' You owe me that even if I did leave my baby with you to keep her safe. Even if I did leave the witness protection program."

He tipped his chin then sat down across from her, his eyes flittering around the room. "She goes by the name Kristin Perry now. Her adoptive parents were Anna and Barton Perry. I handpicked them then pulled a few strings to go through the proper procedures. They were good people."

Eloise swallowed then closed her eyes, trying to imagine what Kristin looked like now. "Were?" she asked, the dread congealing in her stomach.

"They were killed in a car accident several months ago." At her gasp, he held up a hand. "It was a horrible accident, nothing more. Believe me, I had it thoroughly investigated. Anyway, Kristin found something in their things, a sealed envelope with…the note you left me. She got in touch with my brother, Micah—he's a U.S. Marshal now, here in Montana. She didn't know he was my brother but…we had to tell her. I met with her in Billings and warned her off, then later she came to see me in Chicago and while she was there, she attended Vincent Martino's trial."

Eloise put a hand to her mouth. "What are you saying?"

He leaned forward, his fingers templed together. "She knows about you, Eloise. And she was so determined to find you that she almost got herself killed. Vincent is out to get both of you now. And if he's the one who sent those roses, then we have to move you immediately."

The pulse building inside Eloise's temple throbbed into overdrive. A silent prayer screamed throughout her mind as she stared at Jackson. "Dear God, what do I do now? What if he finds Kristin?"

She hadn't realized she'd said it out loud until Jackson's dark eyebrows lifted in a reaction. The phone rang, causing both of them to jump—Eloise in sheer terror and Jackson into high-alert mode.

Jackson put a hand on her arm. "Whoever it is, act normal. Don't give anything away."

She nodded as she went into the kitchen to get the cordless phone. "Hello?"

"Girl, I'm worried about you. Where are you? And where is Meredith? She's not answering her phone. You girls have a late night or something?"

Eloise steadied herself, the image of Meredith's body still fresh in her mind. "Hi, Verdie. I'm sorry. I was feeling kind of sick and I thought it would pass. I should have called you back. I might be a while." She shot Jackson a glance. "If I even make it in."

"Take your time, honey. I called Timothy in for backup since I can't get Meredith on the phone. We're kind of slow today, anyway. Except for this delicious-looking blond-haired, blue-eyed stranger who keeps winking at me, it's just a few of the locals and me, Timothy and Frank. You rest up. Between my old man and that scrawny teenager, we'll take care of things. We got plenty of cinnamon rolls turning brown in the oven and I know how to bake bread and cook French toast, even if you make the best in the world. I just wish Meredith would show her pretty face. I could use her help with Mr. Delicious. The man's already been through a whole pot of coffee and he wants two of those cinnamon rolls."

Eloise didn't comment on Meredith. She couldn't. And she was pretty sure Mr. Delicious was probably one of the FBI agents Jackson was communicating with right now. "Thanks, Verdie. I'll call you later, I promise."

"Okay, then. Hey, are you sure you're all right?"

Eloise wanted to laugh again. She might not ever be all right. "I'm fine. Just a bug or a summer cold."

She hung up then came back to the living room, her knees too weak to keep her standing straight. "My coworker, checking on me again. I rarely miss work." Grabbing the arm of the couch, she managed to fall back against it. The dizziness returned, forcing her to put her head down and close her eyes.

Jackson was beside her before she took her next breath. "You don't look so hot. Are you really sick? Is that why you didn't go to work?"

Eloise didn't dare open her eyes. "I don't feel so hot, either, but I'm okay. And I need to know the rest." She lifted her head but avoided looking directly at him. "Is…Kristin safe?"

"She is. But she's stubborn like her mother. She wouldn't let up. She hired a private investigator to help her track you down. And somebody out there found out about it and tried to harm both of them. But…for now, she's safe. I might as well warn you, though, she wants to see you and if she tries, that could lead Martino right to your door." He stopped, shook his head. "She did see you down in Mountain Springs, at the fair. I was there with her."

"That was just last month." Eloise shot off the couch. "I won the prize for my Huckleberry pie. I used the money to do some quick renovations at my place here." She paced around, holding on to the back of the couch. "You were there? Kristin was there? But why—"

"I couldn't let her talk to you," Jackson explained without really answering her question. "We were being watched by Martino's men, and later we saw him there. It was too risky."

"And now?"

"And now, she knows you're safe and she knows I'm going to make sure of that. She's willing to wait, but not for long. She wants to get to know her mother."

Eloise clutched the couch, her stomach roiling, a white-hot heat of fear flaring through her system. She hadn't managed to eat any breakfast and now she felt empty, so empty. But this emptiness didn't come from lack of nourishment. It came from that deep, gaping hole in her heart. She'd missed out on so many things.

"I can't see her, Jackson. It's too dangerous for her. I can't see her ever."

He got up to come around the couch. "Listen to me.

We're so close to capturing Martino and when we do…it will all be over. You won't have to hide anymore. Then it won't be dangerous for either of you."

"You can't promise me that," she said, anger giving her strength. "You promised me that once before, remember? And I almost lost my baby girl. I gave her up to protect her and I won't change on that. I have to stay away from her for the same reason."

His hand on her arm steadied her, but the warmth she felt from his touch only added to her misery. Because she'd put him in danger, too. He'd die for her; she knew that. And she couldn't have that on her conscience. Not now, when she had yet another threat hanging over her like fog over a mountain. If Jackson found out she'd witnessed Meredith's death, he'd go into double time trying to save her. She couldn't risk the exposure or the scrutiny. Or the guilt that would come if something happened to Kristin or him.

She whirled, gathering her purse as she headed up the stairs. "You're right. I have to leave. I have to get out of here."

"Wait," Jackson called, stomping to the bottom of the stairs. "You can't run away without my help, Eloise. Not this time."

She pivoted to stare down at him. "And you can't come in here and announce *that* after twenty-two years of no other choice, Jackson. I've done nothing but run since the last time I saw you. And you did suggest that I might need to move."

He held on to the banister. "Yes, but just to a safe house. I'm here to see that you don't have to go anywhere permanently again. If you'll let me help you. I'm telling you—you don't have to do this by yourself anymore."

"Yes, I do. I have to protect Kristin. And you."

He followed her to the landing, grabbing her to pull her around. "Don't worry about either of us. Kristin is with a good man now. And he knows how to take care of her."

That declaration floored Eloise. "She's…happy?"

"I think so. His name is Zane Black and he cares about her. He's the P.I. I mentioned. He went through the same thing—he was adopted and he recently found his brother."

"She fell in love with the man who helped her track me down?"

He nodded. "What are the odds?"

His words echoed her earlier thoughts. Eloise knew the odds, though. Hadn't *she* fallen in love with her protector all those years ago? But that love hadn't survived the Mob, even if seeing Jackson again made it feel as strong as ever. She couldn't give in to that notion; she'd just lose him all over again.

Ignoring the keen loneliness that shrouded her soul, Eloise said, "I'm glad she found someone."

"Me, too. Zane is crazy about her and now he has his brother, too."

"Good, then he has his happy ending. And if I leave her alone, maybe Kristin will have one, too."

"She will. They're engaged but she wants you at their wedding."

Eloise closed her eyes, imagining Kristin walking down the aisle, smiling, happy. But then another image came into her mind. That of her daughter lying dead, surrounded by crushed white roses. "I can't go. I won't risk that. As much as I'd love to be there, I won't ruin her special day."

Jackson held her with a hand on her arm, his gaze moving over her face with that same concentration she remembered so well. "You're still stubborn, I see."

She took that as a compliment. "I've learned to take care of myself. I didn't have any other choice."

"I can see that, too, but this is a real threat and we're dealing with a dangerous man. And this time, I'm not letting you go anywhere—not without me."

The phone rang again. Eloise pushed past Jackson to answer it. He followed her back downstairs, a finger to his lips. "Be cool," he cautioned.

Eloise thought her head might split open from trying to be cool. Taking a deep breath, she answered on the third ring. "Hello?"

"It's me again." Verdie. And she sounded strange, her voice raspy.

"What is it?" Eloise asked, fear pouring over her. She could feel the sweat popping out down her spine. She knew what was wrong already. She knew and she was helpless to do anything about it.

"The police were just here, honey." Verdie inhaled a deep sob. "It's about our little Meredith, and it's bad. It's so bad."

"What?" Eloise looked down at the floor, acutely aware that Jackson was hanging on her every word. Her stomach clenched, her heart rate increased. She felt as if she'd just finished a long marathon. But she knew this run was just beginning all over again. "What is it?"

"They found Meredith dead this morning, Ellie. In the woods just beyond her apartment. Two officers were here asking questions. It's awful, just so awful."

Eloise found a chair, managed to sit down. "Oh, no. I can't believe that. I—" She stopped, unable to lie to her friend. "Do they know what happened?"

"No. They asked a lot of questions, took notes. They don't know and if they do, they ain't talking. Her husband is pretty shook up, according to these two. You know he's a cop, remember?"

"I remember." *Shook up.* Eloise remembered seeing Randall Parker last night. He was standing over his wife, crying. He was sorry, all right. Sorry that his unbridled anger and unyielding control had caused him to kill a beautiful young woman. But now, she imagined he was shook up because he had seen someone up on that landing last night. He'd obviously moved the body and now he was probably afraid that person would come forward soon to reveal him as the killer.

Had he already figured out it was her?

"I remember," she said again, her mind screaming the truth. "I'll be right there, Verdie."

"No, don't come. We'll just shut down for the day, if I can get rid of this pretty-boy coffee-slurper. He seems mighty interested in what's going on. Must be one of those crime junkies. It's just so horrible." Verdie sniffed then started crying all over again.

"Get him out of there and close up," Eloise said,

forcing back the tears that would come soon. "I'll come down—"

"Honey, don't bother. The cops are on their way to your house to question you. I gotta go."

Verdie hung up while Eloise stared at the phone. Then she turned to Jackson. "I need to leave, Jackson. Right now. Something's come up at the diner."

But a knock at the door halted that plan.

Jackson summed things up pretty quickly. "What's going on, Eloise? Has someone threatened you already?"

"No," she said, thinking it was useless to lie to him. He'd stay on her until she told him everything. Better to get it out in the open. At least she could trust him— and he did have the authority to help her. She hoped. "I can't say much now, but...something happened last night. Something really bad."

The knocking continued and Duff barked a response to each knock, impatient with all the visitors this morning.

Jackson held his hands on his hips, a frown burrowing across his forehead. "Eloise?"

She pushed toward him, then leaned close. "One of my best friends was killed last night," she said on a whisper. "And I'm pretty sure her husband killed her. I went to help her, but I was too late." Then she explained what Verdie had told her. "That's why I wasn't at work."

Jackson's eyes widened as he processed what she was saying. "Is that the cops at the door? Or him?"

She bobbed her head, then grabbed his arm. "Her

husband *is* a cop. I can't tell them what I know. If I do, he'll come after me. I can't step forward and tell the truth, not now. Maybe not ever. I can't risk it, Jackson. You have to help me."

She watched as he went into action. Clicking his communication device, he asked, "GQ, what's the status at your location?"

The knocks persisted but Jackson held up a hand to keep her still. "Got it. Yes, I just heard. Just get out of there now before you blow your cover."

He lifted a brow toward Eloise, grunted, then sprang toward the door. "Open it," he said, "and answer their questions." Then he whispered a quick command to his team. "Stand down and listen in. Don't move until you hear from me."

With a quick motion, he pulled her toward the door. "Work with me, Eloise. You have to make this look good. Just let them ask their questions but don't give away anything right now." Then he said into her ear, "And after they leave, you'd better tell me everything, so I can make sure you live to see your daughter again."

THREE

Jackson motioned to her again. "Just listen and let them talk. If they ask questions you don't want to answer, tell them you don't know."

She moved her head to indicate she understood. Jackson stood back, holding Duff by his collar. "It's okay, boy." But it wasn't okay and the dog was smart enough to figure that out. Eloise was in trouble, serious trouble. A double threat wasn't good right now. "Go," he said.

She did as he told her, slowly opening the door but keeping the chain on the lock. "Yes?"

"Ellie Smith?"

She bobbed her head. "Yes."

The two officers looked at each other then back to her. Jackson sized them up from his hidden position at the window. They were in plain clothes but they had that weary-eyed cop look. And Eloise hadn't reacted overly much so he didn't think the man she'd accused of murder was standing just outside her door.

"We need to talk to you, ma'am. About your friend Meredith Parker."

"I heard. Verdie called me," she said, her voice quivering.

Another glance between them. "Can we come in?"

She looked at Jackson. He pointed to the tiny down-stairs bathroom then started toward the hallway. "Yes, of course. Let me just calm down my dog and put him away so we can talk." Shutting the door, she turned to Jackson again, motioning for him to take Duff with him. "Duff, go," she said loud enough for the officers to hear her through the door. Then she shooed the dog toward the powder room.

The dog did as she commanded and followed Jackson, but he stayed alert. "Good dog," Jackson said on a low voice to the animal. He left the bathroom door cracked so he'd have a good view of the two men, then nodded to Eloise, his hand stroking Duff's back to keep him inside the room.

Speaking into his radio, he said, "Roark, we have a problem. Listen to me and take notes."

"Got it," Roark shot back.

Eloise opened the front door and stood back, making sure she wasn't in Jackson's line of sight so he could see the two men. "Come in."

The two officers swaggered into the hallway then glanced around. Through the narrow slit of the open powder room door, Jackson sized them up while Duff whined behind him. One was short and stout and the other one was tall and slender. And they both looked nervous. Interesting pair.

"Sorry, we hate to bother you at home but your coworker said you were sick today."

Eloise lifted her head toward the beefy one. "I'm not feeling well. I'm upset about Meredith."

Looking confused, one of the men said, "We're sorry. We need to ask you some questions."

Eloise didn't have to fake the pale color washing over her face. Jackson could tell she was fighting to stay in control. So was he. Even though he was itching to question these two, based on what Eloise had told him about the husband being a cop, he couldn't give away his cover right now. The last thing he needed was a rogue cop trying to cover his own tracks by coming after Eloise. This new wrinkle could mess up their whole operation.

"I'll try to answer any questions," Eloise said, not inviting the men to sit down.

"Meredith Parker was found dead this morning in the woods behind her apartment complex."

They waited, the silence of expectancy filling the room with a palpable tension.

Eloise moved back, reaching out toward a nearby chair. She looked down at the floor, her shoulders hunched as she held tightly to the chair. She was clearly upset, maybe because she hadn't allowed herself to be upset yet and now the reality of her friend's death was hitting her full force.

And Jackson didn't think it was an act.

Eloise closed her eyes, shuddered a breath. "Do you know what happened?"

"We're still investigating that, but…an early-morning jogger found her lying just off the path by a stream. She lived in the complex so we think maybe she went out for a walk and fell and hit her head…or someone attacked her."

"Attacked her? On the path?" Eloise gasped again. "Who would do that to Meredith?"

The way she stood up straight and almost shouted that question alerted Jackson to just how traumatized she really was. And here he'd just sprung the worst on her with all this mess from her past. And the fact that her daughter wanted to see her.

He held his breath, hoping she wouldn't cave. Then he whispered, "Police are here. Employee Meredith Parker. Dead. Husband is a suspect. Subject possible witness to the murder."

Eloise clung to the chair, gulping deep breaths of air. "Do you have any suspects?"

Knowing that his whole team—Roark, Marcus and Thea—were taking down the facts he'd managed to feed to them, Jackson trusted his people would get right on the details of what the local cops had so far. Even though this was out of their hands technically, they'd have to watch this new development and try to figure a way around it.

The skinny one of the two gave Eloise the once-over, then said, "We're still trying to piece things together so we're not calling this a homicide yet. Her husband, Randall, is a member of the Snow Sky police force and he's my partner, so of course, we've put a special priority on this." He leaned close, his tone condescending. "You might know that Detective Parker is a lieutenant in the police department. And a well-respected man."

Eloise nodded. "Yes, I'm aware of that. He came by the bakery a lot—to see her."

Jackson read that as "to check up on her" and even

from where he stood in another room, he felt the tension radiating off of Eloise's body as she said the words. He didn't like the way the patrol officer had informed her of Randall Parker's rank—almost as if it was some kind of warning—or threat.

"What can I do to help?" Eloise said, still shocked, probably because even though she'd witnessed this murder she hadn't wanted to believe it. Now it was very real. She couldn't go back or run away.

"We just need to ask you some questions," Beefy said. "When was the last time you saw Meredith Parker?"

Eloise let out a breath then inhaled again. "Yesterday when we left work."

"You mean when you both left Ellie's—the café and bakery where you both work?"

"Yes, I'm the owner. Meredith is—was—a waitress. She's worked for me about two years. They moved here from Great Falls."

Jackson took in that bit of information. Had someone come after the waitress thinking she was Eloise? And why did Eloise seem so sure the detective had killed his own wife? She'd said she was there, but could she be wrong? The body had been found in the woods. Keeping his eyes on the two men, he ignored the tension ripping through his neck and shoulders. This situation would bring unwanted scrutiny to Eloise. And the press could bring Vincent Martino into town.

"So you saw her leave?"

"We walked out together. She got in her car and I—I had my dog with me. He always comes to work with me. I walk to work and back since it's not that far.

I waved goodbye to her—" Her voice cracked. "That was the last time—"

"I know this is hard, but just think back and tell us anything you think might help," Skinny said on a solicitous note.

She glanced up at him, obviously surprised at the sudden kindness. "I'm trying. I can't imagine who would want to harm Meredith. She was so sweet, you know. All golden-haired and blue-eyed. The perfect California girl who moved to Montana to get away from the Los Angeles crowd." She heaved a sob, her hand at her mouth. Her gaze swept over the two men. "And now…*she's dead*."

Jackson figured she'd given Meredith's description and some background for his sake, so his team could get right on things. Smart woman. Too smart. The way she'd emphasized "she's dead" when she'd looked at the officers didn't bode well. If she didn't end this soon, she'd accuse the whole police department of being in on this murder. And maybe she was right about that.

"Do you need to sit down?" the officer asked, his words still gentle. But the quick look he gave the other officer hadn't been so kind.

"No," she replied, sharp and clear. "I want to know what happened to my friend. Can you two tell me that?"

"We don't know," Skinny said. "That's why we're asking questions. Lieutenant Parker has been up half the night, interrogating anyone he can find, looking for witnesses. He wants to find out what happened to his wife."

"That's good," Eloise said, her voice deadly calm now. "I hope he finds whoever did this."

"Trust me, he will. If someone harmed his wife, that person will pay. He's devastated. Just devastated."

Eloise buried her head in her hands. Was she praying for guidance or plotting her own way to avenge this murder? Jackson couldn't be sure.

"What else can I do?" she asked, her tone determined.

Beefy looked at Eloise for a few heartbeats. "Ms. Smith, is there anything else you can think of—say, someone who came in the bakery and had words with Meredith? Anybody who'd want to hurt her?"

Her head came up and Jackson knew she was very close to going ballistic. "Meredith Parker was one of the nicest, sweetest girls I've ever known. She went to church every Sunday and she was a favorite with all our customers, so no, I can't think of anyone—" She stopped, her fingers holding on to the chair with an iron grip. "I can't think why anyone would want to hurt her. She was a good person."

Skinny finally stepped forward. "I think that's enough for now. You're in shock. We'll give you some space and maybe you'll remember something else later."

Jackson didn't like the way Skinny's gaze darted around the room. What was he trying to hide? What did he already know? The kid was as nervous and jumpy as a squirrel.

Beefy looked skeptical but Skinny handed her a card. "Call us if you do remember anything. The captain's got the whole team on this. Meredith was like one of our own, you know."

"I understand that," Eloise said with the same determined tone she'd used for most of the conversation. Then she lifted her head and glared at them. "Give my condolences to Lieutenant Parker, please."

"We will, ma'am. Thanks for your time."

She opened the door to let the men out. "Officers," she called, causing both of them to glance around, "if someone did kill Meredith, I hope you do everything you can to find that person. Can you promise me that?"

Both men nodded. "We intend to do just that," Skinny replied.

After she shut the door, Eloise hurried toward the couch then fell down on it, her head in her hands again.

Jackson came out of the bathroom, Duff close on his heels. He sat down beside her then pulled her into his arms to hold her close for a minute. "Are you trying to get yourself killed? You almost spilled the truth right then and there."

"I want justice," she said, her paleness turning to a rush of color as anger poured through her. The flush only emphasized the scar near her lips. "I've been running from crime for over half my life, Jackson. And I want justice, just this once, for Meredith. I know he killed her. I didn't see him push her, but he was standing over her body and the only reason he's out there searching for witnesses is to cover this murder. He moved her to the woods and just left her there. He'll do anything to keep his dirty secret and to keep his standing in the department. But I'm going to do everything in my power to make sure he gets what he deserves, even if it means I have to come out of hiding to do it."

An hour later, Jackson sat across from her, waiting on a report from Roark. He'd sent the team back to the apartment they'd rented across the way. By now, Theresa Romaro would be doing a thorough background check on Randall and Meredith Parker. Theresa, or Thea, as Roark liked to call her, was a hotshot computer expert and an asset in the field. She'd find out anything they needed to know on Randall Parker. And she'd find out about who sent those roses, too, since he'd given her the rundown on that.

"So we just sit here?" Eloise asked, her gaze moving around the cozy, sparse den.

"For now. It's okay. You've been through a horrible shock."

She glared at him, her eyes saying what she couldn't voice. Disbelief, shock, worry and regret. It was there.

"I should go to the café. I need to be with my employees."

"They're all safe at home now," he said. "Roark made sure of that."

"Did he—"

"He tailed Verdie and Frank and had Thea watch the kid home. They're all okay. And no, you don't need to go to the café. You don't need to talk to the press or get your picture in the paper or on the evening news."

She picked up a big blue tote bag then pulled out some knitting needles and yarn. "So I just sit here?"

"Until I decide what to do next, yes."

She shot him a look full of doubt and anger. Then she lowered her gaze. "I should be glad you showed up. I was paralyzed with fear all night. I don't like that feeling." She shook her head. "I'd almost gotten too complacent here, thinking I was finally safe."

He leaned forward. "I know it's hard, having to go through this again. But I'm glad I'm here, too. And we're going to take care of all of this."

She didn't look so sure, but she gave him a quiet nod.

Jackson looked away then took in the bright colors of the furniture. While there wasn't much of it, what pieces she had arranged were bright and cheery. She liked reds and blues, apparently. And she'd incorporated some Native American and Wild West art into the mix. But she didn't have any family pictures anywhere. None. That broke his heart. And he had to wonder if she had any real friends.

"What are you knitting?"

She looked up, her hands holding the yellow yarn against the big hooked needles. "Baby caps. We sponsor a children's home at my church. They always need warm caps for the newborns and…for the babies that are adopted out."

Her eyes held his for a minute then she went back to her knitting. Jackson didn't know what to say. She grieved for her own child but she helped others with this small offering in order to assuage that grief. His heart felt too heavy inside his chest. Way too heavy.

So he focused on his job.

"As soon as I get more details, we'll form a plan," he said, taking a sip of his fourth cup of coffee. It was enough for now that he had her in his sights and he didn't plan on letting her out of his sight until she was finally safe. "I should hear something soon."

"So," she said on a note of resignation, "tell me about this task force."

He took out his phone to check messages. "I told you."

"No, you told me about the women who've been murdered and you've brought me up to speed on the Martino case. You have a mysterious informant and you think you have a leak and you told me all of this because I'm the reason for those murders and you want me to take this seriously. But I need to know about these people you handpicked to help you. What if I can't trust them?"

"You can or I wouldn't have them here with me," he replied, his pulse tripping into overdrive because of her distrust and her perpetual fear. He was going to end this so he could see her smile again. And even though he didn't rely on anyone for much of anything, he did ask God to show him how to do that. Jackson didn't know how to pray but maybe it was time he learned.

For her sake, at least.

"I'm waiting," she said, impatience slicing through her words. Before he could respond, she said, "I see you haven't changed much. Still don't like to carry on a casual conversation."

"I wouldn't call this casual," he retorted, concern for her making him edgy. "We have a big problem here, Eloise. You managed to leave your house on foot, right under the noses of my agents. You could have been killed, too."

"Like I don't get that." She got up, moved around the room. "I can't stand this. I should be with Verdie and Frank. They loved Meredith."

"Sit down and I'll tell you anything you want to know."

She stilled but she didn't sit. "Just talk to me, Jackson, just to keep me from falling apart, okay?"

"Okay."

He told her about Roark's habit of calling him Big Mac. And about the time Roark had pushed him into a garbage bin to keep him from getting shot. He told her about Marcus Powell's penchant for fancy duds and how he got the name GQ because he always looked like he'd stepped out of the pages of a magazine.

"He was the one at the bakery, wasn't he?" she asked, telling him what Verdie had said about the blue-eyed, blond-haired man hanging around.

"Yes."

"And Theresa? What's she like?"

The question was so innocent, yet so telling. He was sure Eloise craved female friendship. And now, one of the few friends she had was dead. That seemed to be a pattern in her life—death all around her. And fear.

"Theresa is solid. She grew up in a bad neighborhood

back in Chicago, but she was determined to become somebody. She made it out by the skin of her teeth, but not before she witnessed her brother's murder. Drug dealers. She went to the authorities and gave them a statement that helped put the dealers away for a long time, then she left Chicago. She didn't come back until the day she showed up in my office, fresh from the academy. She wants to get rid of all the bad guys and she's good at her job. Plus, she comes in handy when I'm dealing with difficult women."

Eloise's head came up at that remark. But her lips twisted at his sarcasm. "Am I being difficult?"

"You have every reason to be difficult."

"What are the odds, huh?"

"Something like that." He glanced at his list of voice messages and saw his brother, Micah, had called. "I told you about Micah, right?"

"Your little brother," she said. "I remember him."

"What are the odds of him winding up on this task force, too," he replied. "Small world, full of coincidences."

"Maybe you two getting back together this way wasn't a coincidence," she said, her knitting needles never breaking stride.

His cell rang before he had time to analyze her words. "Talk to me," he said.

Theresa's cool voice lifted through the airwaves. "Your man Parker was apparently married once before, sir. And that wife went missing. They found her dead in a ravine just east of Great Falls. Her murder was never solved."

"How long ago?"

"Five years. He got married again—to Meredith Grigsby, and they left that area and came here. Moved up in rank pretty quickly once he joined the Snow Sky Police Department."

"Anything else?"

"Not much for now. He has a clean record but he's been through some anger management training for roughing up suspects and perps."

"Maybe we should add wives to that list, too."

"That's what I'm thinking. Meredith is clean. Nothing there. Not even a speeding ticket. Oh, and I'm still trying to find out where the roses came from. So far, no luck there."

"Good work, Thea. Keep me posted."

He hung up to stare over at Eloise. "Did you know Parker had been married before?"

"No." Her eyebrows lifted in surprise. "Meredith never mentioned it."

"Probably because she didn't know."

"They'd only been married about three years."

"His first wife was found dead in a ravine over in Great Falls."

She sank back down, shock and rage causing her to start that back-and-forth rocking again. "I tried to get her away. She'd come to work with bruises, but she always had an excuse. She was so afraid of him."

"Did he ever harass her at work?"

"No, never. But he came by every day to visit. She said he was making sure she was where she was supposed to be. At first, she thought that was considerate.

Then she realized he was paranoid and controlling. He didn't want her to work so he kept tabs on her all the time."

"Does he know that you were aware of his abuse?"

"No. We were careful. I came close to telling him off a couple of times, but I stopped myself—to protect her."

"Wise move. What was the plan?"

"You mean, about getting her away?"

Jackson nodded, drained his coffee.

"I was supposed to pick her up while he was on a stakeout last night. He rarely called her when he was on a late-night job. He just set the alarm and dared her to leave the house. We had everything arranged, though. She learned how to reset the alarm to make it look like she was home. I'd rented a car and hidden it in her apartment complex. I planned to walk to her apartment at midnight and get her, then drive her to the bus station so she could get to a shelter in Billings. By the time he figured things out, she'd be long gone. Only, he came home early. He got there before I did. And I guess they had words. She called me in a panic to come and help her. I ran out of my apartment and all the way to her house."

"Do you have any idea why he came home?"

"I don't know. Maybe he was onto us the whole time or maybe he got suspicious last night. Maybe he forgot something. He's a smart man, Jackson. He won't stop until he finds out who saw him last night."

"We won't let him get to you."

"He knows everything about me. Or at least, he

knows the 'new' me—Ellie Smith. But the man can dig up just about anything and he'd like nothing better than to use what he finds."

"Such as—you being in the Witness Protection Program."

She nodded. "If he finds that out—he'd sell me to the highest bidder. Then he could wash his hands of Meredith's death…and me."

Jackson got up to stand in front of her. "That's why we're going to get you out of here tonight."

"I thought you didn't want me to run again."

"You're not going to run. You're going to take a vacation—with my team and me. You're grieving your friend's death."

She glared at him, her eyes wide. "I *am* grieving. I want to go to her funeral. I have to. He'll suspect something if I don't. I have to, Jackson."

"That won't happen until we get the autopsy report and have the all clear. And I'll be there with you, understand. That way I can protect you and watch him at the same time. For now, if anyone asks, my cover will be that I'm a good friend who's helping you through your grief. Then you'll make it known that you're going to stay with some friends for a while, just to get away."

She nodded, her arms crossed in a defensive gesture. "It *will* be hard to go back to work. I guess this could work for a while at least."

"And in the meantime, we'll find the evidence we need to get him."

"You're going to be one busy man, trying to protect me from him and the Mob."

"I'll manage."

Another knock sounded at the door.

Since she'd put Duff in the fenced-in yard out back, no warning barks sounded through the quiet room. Jackson nodded toward the door. "See who it is."

Eloise looked through the peephole then spun around toward Jackson, a hand to her throat. "It's him. It's Randall Parker."

Adrenaline rushed through Jackson. "He probably just wants to talk to you, but—"

"But he might be here to make sure I never talk. Should I let him in?"

Before Jackson could answer, Randall Parker banged on the door again, this time in several rapid-fire beats followed by a message full of rage. "Open up, Ellie. I know you're in there. I have some questions for you. And I'm not leaving until you answer them, you hear me?"

Jackson shook his head. "Don't say a word."

A fist hit the door again then Randall Parker spewed several expletives. "You think you can hide from me, Ms. Smith? You have no idea what I can do." He hit the door again. "You know something about Meredith. I know you do. Let me in or I'll tear this door down."

Then Eloise did something that threw Jackson completely off guard. She found her purse on the coffee table and pulled out a gun. And she had that gun aimed toward the front door.

Moving behind her, Jackson put his fingers against his own gun, his eyes on Eloise. "Don't do it," he said on a hiss of a whisper. "Eloise, do you hear me?"

"I won't let him kill anybody else," she replied, resolve and determination in her own forced whisper.

Jackson touched a hand to her arm. "We'll get him. But not this way. Do you hear me?"

She shuddered, her knuckles white against the gun. Then she slowly nodded. "What am I supposed to do, Jackson? Can you tell me that?"

"Let him go for now."

From somewhere in the backyard, Duff's loud barks pierced the late-morning air. Eloise whirled. "He must have gone around back!"

Jackson didn't wait to find out. Quickly, he informed the team of the situation. Then he turned to Eloise.

"This is about to get ugly," he told her. "Gather your things."

"Why?"

"Change of plans. We're getting you out of here today."

FOUR

Eloise couldn't move. Still holding the gun, she stared at Jackson. "How will we get away?"

Jackson nodded toward the back door. "First, we wait him out to make sure he doesn't try to outrun Duff. After he's gone and we're clear, we'll make plans to leave. I'll make sure the word gets out about you shutting down the café."

Eloise listened to Duff's barking. "And if he gets in here?"

"If he does break in, then we'll try a different tactic."

"Such as?"

"Such as me waiting to greet him."

That scenario made Eloise feel better, but she didn't let go of her gun. Duff's barking became more frantic and more dangerous. "Even if he gets through the gate, he can't get past Duff."

"I agree. Just stay there and, Eloise, give me the gun."

She glanced at Jackson then looked down at the gun she held clenched in one hand, wondering if she had the courage to actually fire it. She could shoot through the door and take care of Parker, but then where would that get her? She'd never get to see her daughter if she did that. And yet, right now, it was so tempting. "I've carried concealed guns for a long, long time. I know how to use one."

"I understand that, but…you can't do this. Not here, not today."

"Why not? If I go to prison, at least I'd be safe, right?"

"Not really," he replied. "And you don't want to go to prison."

"No, because I've been living in my own prison since the day I last saw you and my baby. Maybe it's time to just come out of hiding, once and for all."

"And what would Kristin think if I have to tell her that her mother murdered a man in cold blood, out of rage and revenge?"

Eloise thought about that and the shame of it almost brought her to her knees. Her whole body stiffened but she finally held out the gun, barrel down, toward Jackson. "Here, take it." She glared at him, wishing he'd never come back into her life even as she thanked God that he had. "But I want it back."

"Okay."

Jackson came toward her, his eyes steady on hers, his hand out. He took the gun and carefully shoved it under his belt. Then he pulled her close, wrapping his arms around her, holding her, not in a hard, guarded way, but in a protective, gentle way. His touch and his nearness almost unraveled her carefully controlled rage and pain.

Eloise closed her eyes, listening to Duff's furious barks and snarls. She prayed for so many things, but mostly she asked God to protect Jackson and her daughter. And to help her find the courage to do what needed to be done.

Jackson didn't move. He wrapped his arms around her then tugged her head down onto his shoulder. He seemed to become a human shield between her and the back door. Finally, Eloise heard the rattling of the locked gate to the backyard and then she heard a car crank up and zoom away, tires squealing with frustration.

"He's gone," she whispered into Jackson's spicy-smelling lapel.

"So he is. You're safe for now."

"I want to be safe forever."

"I'm working on that."

An hour later, Thea tapped on the front door. After calming Duff and making sure no one was lurking about outside, Jackson motioned her in. "Shoot to kill," he ordered, explaining that only FBI task force agents were allowed through the door.

Thea nodded, her dark thick curls bobbing. "I understand, sir."

Jackson turned to where Eloise sat rigid on the couch. "Eloise, this is agent Theresa Romaro—we call her Thea. She's going to stay here with you while I check on a few things."

Eloise gave Thea a quick, curt nod and a halfhearted smile. "Hello."

Thea walked over to the couch. "Hi, Ms. Smith. How you doing?"

"Not so good," Eloise said, rubbing her arms. "It's been a long day."

"I hear that," Thea said on a breezy note. "I'm here now, so if you need to rest—"

"I can't rest."

Jackson shot Thea a look. "Just watch and wait. I'll be back as soon as I can."

Thea nodded, glancing down at Duff. Holding her knuckles out toward the dog, she said, "Got it."

Jackson went over to Eloise. "I'd like to get you away from here immediately, but we have some logistics to work out. We'll leave at midnight."

"Can I take Duff?"

The whispered request got to him. He swallowed. "Of course. I'm thinking of making Duff an honorary FBI agent."

That brought a smile to her face and a grunt from Duff. The big dog lay curled up by Eloise's feet, his doleful eyes alert as he sniffed toward Thea.

Giving Eloise one last look, Jackson headed for the door. "I'll be back soon."

Thea followed him to secure the alarm. "Roark and GQ are waiting. And we're still digging for more information on Detective Parker."

"Thanks." Jackson opened the door and left, his head up, his gaze roaming the secluded neighborhood. It was a nice summer night and he could hear people out on boats in the lake just beyond the park. Was one of those people watching the apartment, just waiting for the right opportunity to make a move?

He didn't want to leave Eloise, but he had to secure a safe house and he didn't want her listening to orders and getting all worked up while he did so. Her first instinct this morning had been to run, but now because of her grief about her friend's death and her need to play it cool with Parker, she wasn't too keen on leaving Snow Sky. But he wasn't too keen on letting her hide away in that tiny town house, either. If Parker thought she knew something, he'd be back and from what Jackson had seen and heard about the man, he'd be even angrier on the second visit than he'd been this morning. He'd already paid a visit to her friend Verdie, demanding information, according to Verdie's last phone call. Eloise had told him that Verdie was afraid of Parker, and with good reason.

But Verdie had also told Eloise she had Frank to protect her. Frank and a big shotgun. Verdie had been worried about Eloise being alone. He'd allowed Eloise to explain to Verdie that she had a concerned friend staying with her. That had satisfied Verdie for now.

He wasn't so sure Randall Parker would be satisfied, however, until he talked to Eloise.

Making one more visual sweep of the townhomes, trees and grassy parks beyond the buildings, Jackson let out the breath he'd been holding. So far, so good. He quietly let himself into the apartment where Roark and Marcus sat hunched over computers and surveillance cameras.

"What's the latest?" he asked, automatically heading to the coffeepot sitting on the kitchen counter.

"We're trying to secure the official crime-scene reports on Parker's first wife. Our agent in Great Falls is working on that right now. But you know how it is—the locals are doing the 'Who wants to know?' routine."

Jackson didn't say anything. They were trying to keep this on the down-low to avoid exposure. He slurped his coffee, the memory of holding Eloise in his arms front and center in his mind.

"Hey, Big Mac, you need to eat," Roark reminded him, pointing to the soggy pizza on the counter.

Jackson stared at the pepperonis and mushrooms, his stomach growling while his mind rejected biting into the mushy mess. "I'll eat later. Anything on Martino?"

"No, sir," GQ said, his white shirtsleeves rolled up and his silk tie discarded. "All's quiet on that front. All we have to go on for now is that sighting at the fair, but we believe Martino is here with his merry gang of followers. He might send them all to a watery grave for messing up his operation so badly." Then he handed Jackson a list. "Here're the names of his two top capos. We think they both might be here, too."

Jackson memorized the two names—Harry Conyers and Ernest Valenti. He recognized both but that didn't help much right now. His angst hit tenfold each time he thought about the mysterious woman who'd been feeding him tidbits of information for months now, but refused to show her face. He'd been meeting with her once or twice a month over the last few months,

sometimes inside his office back in Chicago and sometimes out near Lake Michigan, sitting on park benches
or near one of the marinas. She always wore a hat,
darkly tinted glasses and a heavy scarf or veil to hide
her face. Very old-world and very Mafia. He'd often
suspected it might be Vincent Martino's long-lost sister
but so far, he couldn't substantiate that hunch. And right
now, he couldn't focus on identifying his informant—
since he'd promised the woman he wouldn't expose
her identity. But he would use what little information
the woman could offer. Maybe she'd at least verify that
these two top capos were here. It was a start.

Martino was growing bolder with each move and
now he had the added distraction of an abusive cop
who might have murdered his wife. Lifting an eyebrow,
he asked, "Do we have *anything* on *anybody?* Surely
someone besides our team has spotted Martino's goons
somewhere in the state of Montana."

"It's a big state, sir," Roark reminded him with
one eyebrow raised in return, which only irritated
Jackson even more. To make amends for mimicking
his boss, Roark added, "You'll feel better if you eat
something."

"I'm fine," Jackson replied, his tone indicating that
subject needed to be dropped. "How are we on securing
a safe house near Great Falls?"

"Affirmative on that," Marcus said, lifting out of his
chair to hand Jackson a document. "Here's the map and
the location."

Jackson scanned the sheet for several minutes
then handed it back to Marcus, watching as Marcus

automatically pushed it through the shredder sitting by the desk. "You checked it thoroughly when you drove over there earlier?"

"Yes, sir. Vacation house of some rich New Yorker. Hefty price for weekly rentals, however. But…we got it for a sweet deal. Gotta love the U.S. government."

Roark and Marcus had gone over to Great Falls and met with the local FBI field agent there—feeding him information on a need-to-know basis to protect Eloise. Jackson had to trust that the house had been swept for bugs and cameras and was indeed set up with a security system and good vantage points.

"It's isolated, hard to find, off the beaten path," Roark said, his hands moving in sweeping gestures with each description. "A nice mountain retreat. Very private." He lifted his eyebrow again.

"Meaning?" Jackson asked, both eyebrows lifted this time. They had this eyebrow-lifting war on a regular basis, but Jackson always won in the end. And tonight, he was tired of playing so he just glared at Roark.

"Oh, nothing." Roark stretched in defeat, got up to pop a soda can open. "Just that…well, we all know this case is very personal for you, sir."

"Meaning?" Jackson asked again, dare in the one word.

"Meaning," Roark continued, not even blinking, "that we know you care about Eloise Hill and her daughter and that you want to get Martino and that…maybe you might have a chance to get the girl that got away—if you don't lose your cool."

"You think so?" Jackson asked, his smile deceptively soft. "You got me all figured out, huh, Agent Canfield?"

Roark knew when to quit. "Uh, well…I hope so, sir."

"Get back to work," Jackson replied, but it was without malice. And he really didn't want to discuss all the variables of this case, especially the alleged rumors floating around the team about how he'd fallen for Eloise all those years ago. It was the truth, but Jackson had neither confirmed nor denied the rumors. And he wasn't going to do so now, either. Not tonight. Maybe not ever.

The goal was to make sure he kept Eloise alive.

Anything past that was too much to hope for right now.

His cell vibrated. Turning away from the quizzical stares of Roark and GQ, he said, "Hello?"

"Hey. Just checking in."

"Micah? How are you?" Jackson tried to keep his half brother updated since Micah, a U.S. Marshal in Billings, also had a vested interest in this case. Micah was part of the task force Jackson had assembled a few months back when they'd finally figured out Martino was behind several unexplained killings—and that they had a leak somewhere helping to fuel that particular fire.

"I'm okay," Micah replied. "How's Mountain Hill?"

The new code name they'd picked for Eloise now that they'd located her. "New developments on that. I'll fill you in." Jackson gave Micah a briefing, knowing he could trust his younger brother. Micah was working day and night with two other agents to find a leak they'd pinpointed as possibly coming from Micah's office.

"Wow," Micah said after hearing Jackson's update. "That is a new wrinkle. Need reinforcements?"

"Negative. I need you to keep working on other areas. I'll keep you posted."

"I have something for you," Micah said. "You know that situation we've been trying to figure?"

"About that leaky faucet?" Jackson asked, referring to the leak they'd been trying to pin down for months.

"Yep. I think I might have found a possible source."

"And?"

"I'd like to send you my findings. Just wanted to give you a heads-up."

"Got it. Patch it through."

He hung up and turned to Roark. "Watch for an incoming from the U.S. Marshal's office, regarding the leak. Top Priority."

Both Roark and Marcus nodded. If they could nail down the person inside the Marshal's office who'd been giving information to the Martino family, that would be half the battle. And it might lead them to Martino before he found Eloise.

"Will we have access if the leak is found?" Marcus asked, his wry smile serenely deceptive.

"Since the Marshal's office put me in charge with this entire case, yes, we'll have a crack at whoever this is, I promise," Jackson responded.

"Good," Marcus said. "This has ruined my plans for a nice summer vacation in the Bahamas."

"Sorry to inconvenience you," Jackson retorted. He walked over to the cold pizza, grabbed a small slice and slowly chewed on it, each bite tasting bland and cold in his mouth. It hit his stomach, heavy and spicy, and sat there like a ten-pound hot pepper. Not good, mixing pizza with too much coffee. Also not good, mixing his feelings for Eloise with trying to crack a complicated case and save an even more complicated witness.

Time to get down to business. And keep it that way. "Let's go over the details of tonight's move," he said, tossing the rest of the pizza slice into the trash.

Eloise tried to read, but she kept staring at the same words until her eyes bleared and the words seemed to dip and sway across the page. She tried to watch television while she knitted, but the local news had a thorough update on the death of Detective Randall Parker's young wife, Meredith. And the cameras had shown Ellie's Café in detail, including sound bites from customers and Verdie and Frank, too. Thea had quickly turned that off.

Now they just sat, Thea reading through files and working on a laptop while Eloise stared at the empty fireplace, her prayers coming all jumbled and errant, her thoughts scattering in the dark recesses of her tired mind.

"Thank you, Theresa," she finally said. "For being here."

"Call me Thea," the young girl said. She had big

brown eyes that sparkled each time she smiled. She was tiny but sturdy and sinewy, her skin color a mix of olive and dark sand. When she talked, her tight curls crinkled and swung around her face each time she moved her head.

"Thea. I like that. Jackson speaks highly of you."

"And you, too," Thea said. Then she looked embarrassed. "I'm not supposed to say things like that."

"I won't tell," Eloise replied. Then because she couldn't stop herself, she said, "What did he tell you about me?"

Thea shut her laptop then looked down at the floor. "I'm not at liberty to discuss that, ma'am."

"I see." Eloise picked up a magazine. "I suppose there's nothing to tell, anyway."

Silence. Then Thea said, "We studied the original case, of course. We know he protected you back in Chicago."

Memories of that time hit Eloise with all the force of an avalanche. "Yes, he certainly did."

The minutes ticked by, then Thea said, "And, ma'am, this is just between you and me, but we—the team—we think he blames himself for…what happened to you. He's never said that, mind you, because he's not one to talk about himself much, good or bad, but—"

Eloise looked up, about to protest. But a noise near the side of the house startled both of them and caused Duff to jump up and pivot in barking circles.

Thea went from sweet young lady to an FBI agent in a fast second, pulling out her weapon as she motioned to Eloise. "Get down behind the couch, please, ma'am."

Eloise did as the woman asked, her heart tripping beats. She called Duff to her, glad the big dog had once again done his job. Since they had only one low lamp on between them, the living room was fairly dark.

Dark enough for them to see a huge shadow hulking near the window by the front door.

"The alarm's on," Eloise said on a whisper. "It should trip if anyone tries to break in."

Thea nodded. Then they both looked up at the alarm pad near the door. And watched as the green indication light suddenly went dark.

And then the whole room went dark, too.

Someone had cut the power.

FIVE

"Ms. Smith?"

"I'm okay, Thea. Duff is with me."

"Stay there," Thea said, her tone no-nonsense.

Eloise could hear the agent moving around. Then she heard, "Sir, we have a situation. A prowler."

Eloise breathed a sigh of relief and sent up a prayer of thanks for electronic communication gadgets. Jackson would be here soon. But, she thought with determination, if he somehow didn't make it, she wouldn't go down without a fight.

She was just so tired of hiding and worrying. But now, she reminded herself, things had changed. Now, her daughter was waiting to see her.

Her eyes slowly adjusted to the dark enough for her to make out Thea's form roaming throughout the downstairs. Thea continued to communicate with the rest of the team, whispering, "Yes, sir," and, "Got it, sir," with each step.

"No sign of anyone trying to break in the front," Thea said, turning in a circle as she held up her weapon and did a continuing scan of the building.

Then Thea stopped. "Upstairs?"

Eloise gulped a breath. There was no way anyone could get to her upstairs bedroom or bath. The windows were tiny and very high. That was one of the reasons she'd liked this place. She had a rope ladder to use in case she had to exit through one of the tight windows, but someone would have to go to a lot of trouble with a rope or very big ladder to climb up.

Watching Thea rush toward the banister, Duff went wild with barking and took off on his own, leaping over the stairs.

"On my way," Thea said. She followed the dog, but called to Eloise, "Special Agent McGraw is at the front door, ma'am."

Eloise heard the knock but couldn't seem to find the strength to get to the door. Then she heard Jackson's voice. "Ellie, let me in."

He'd called her Ellie. It sounded strange coming from him. Her practical mind said he'd done it in case anyone suspicious was still around. Her heart said he'd used it as a term of endearment, since he'd called her that a couple of times long, long ago.

"Ellie?"

Eloise snapped out of her shock and fear and ran for the door, opening it only to have Jackson and two other agents rushing toward her and pushing her back. Duff was back downstairs, clearly confused as to whom he was supposed to protect.

The door shut with a thud as they scattered with flashlights, Jackson issuing orders even as he pulled Eloise close and hurried her into the safety of the kitchen. "Get down."

She followed his lead, crouching behind the counter. Jackson immediately blocked her body with his, his gun drawn as he held his hand on her head.

Then he shouted orders. "Roark, upstairs with Thea. GQ, back door. Take the dog."

The agents dispersed, their footsteps hitting the floor with rapid precision, Duff's paws tapping right behind the one Jackson had called GQ.

Jackson did one more scan then turned on his knees to look at her.

Eloise breathed again, her eyes following the soft glow of Jackson's flashlight. "I'm okay."

He looked her over, his measured gaze telling her he wasn't so sure about that. "What did you hear or see?"

She quickly told him what had happened. "The alarm is silent but it should have alerted the police."

"Not if the intruder knew what he was doing."

She gasped. "A detective would know how to disarm it so it wouldn't send a distress signal."

"Yes, or a Mafia thug. Although the few Martino sent ahead early on weren't that clever."

"But Martino is," she said, glancing up the dark stairs. The whole house had gone deadly quiet. She could hear Duff's occasional barks coming from the tiny backyard.

She stared up at Jackson, anger igniting a raging fire in her belly. "I want this to end, Jackson. One way or another. I can't live like this anymore, not since you told me about Kristin. I can't. It's too dangerous for her and for you."

"I told you not to worry about either of us," he said, his hand coming up to push a long strand of hair off her face. "Kristin is safe. And soon, you'll be picking out a dress for her wedding. Then I'll take you to see her get married, I promise."

She looked up at him, her heart swelling with longing and need. "Jackson…"

"Sir?"

Jackson let her go. Eloise turned to find the dark-haired agent and Thea standing on the landing looking down on them. "What?"

"Intruder got away." The agent hopped down the stairs then pointed when the one called GQ rushed through the back door. "But GQ found something near the bedroom window."

Eloise focused on the tiny, tightly wound cable the agent had coiled over his jacket sleeve. A nylon climbing rope with a metal grabble hook attached to it. She'd seen a few of those kinds of ropes around here since mountain climbing was popular in Montana. But…most mountain climbers also used harnesses and carabiners, or beaners as the locals called them, to link themselves up a mountain.

Jackson hit the nearby wall with a fist. "Someone was trying to climb up the side of the building?"

"It appears that way," Roark said.

"I didn't get a good look, sir," Thea said. "He ran away just as I reached the window and looked down. I think the dog's barking upstairs scared him off."

GQ put away his gun but kept the rope tight against his jacket. "Same here. Just a shadow. He was dressed in black and wearing a sock hat. He slipped over the fence and was gone before I could catch up. I looked up and down the street behind the alley, but...nothing."

"And apparently he dropped his rock-climbing equipment," Jackson said on a sarcastic note of frustration. "We'll have to dust it for prints, but I'm guessing he was wearing gloves, too."

"Probably," Roark echoed in a quiet response. "We might pull some fibers or hair from the rope."

Eloise stared at the bright red rope and the wicked-looking black grabble hook. "Detective Parker is an avid rock and mountain climber," she said. "He'd have access to this type of equipment."

"Him and about every other person in Montana," Roark pointed out.

"It's a start," Jackson replied. "Let's have it analyzed as soon as possible and since we can't bring in a response team from the local police force or use any local labs, we'll have to make sure that evidence makes it to Great Falls with us, understand?"

The three agents nodded.

"We need a large trash bag to put that in," Jackson said.

"I'll get one," Thea offered.

"Under the sink in the kitchen," Eloise replied, her voice low and cautious. She couldn't get the image of that grabble hook out of her mind. If she'd been alone, upstairs— She tried not to think about that. Duff would have tried to protect her, but...all kinds of things could happen with an intruder. Why did she ever believe she might actually be safe here?

"Where's Duff?" Eloise asked, craning her head toward the back door while Thea and Marcus bagged the rope and the hook.

"I thought he was right behind me," the one named Marcus—GQ—replied. "I'll go let him in."

Eloise hurried toward the back door, but Jackson was right behind her. "You can't go out there. Let Marcus check for Duff."

She waited at the door, relieved to see her dog sniffing around at something on the ground near the fence. Marcus walked the perimeters of the yard one more time, stopped and stooped, his flashlight highlighting whatever Duff had found.

Using his jacket to avoid fingerprints, he scooped up the object, then headed toward the door with the stark-white bundle. "I found this, sir. The dog was sniffing at it. Intruder must have dropped it."

Jackson lifted his flashlight to see. "Flowers?" He turned to Eloise. "Roses, Ellie."

Eloise looked into the white tissue and gasped, her heart beating so rapidly she thought it might explode. "White roses," she said, her hand automatically going to her scar. "White roses again, Jackson."

Seeing her obvious distress, Jackson brought his hand up to her shoulder. "Just like the other ones you received at work, right?"

"What's the deal with the roses?" Roark asked.

She stared at the bundle of fat, lush roses. "Vincent Martino's father grew white roses, white with pink-tinged petals." She pointed to the roses Marcus held then pulled her finger back, afraid to even touch the delicate, fat blossoms. "I got some the other day at work."

Her gaze locked with Jackson's. His frown told her things were getting worse. "Someone's certainly trying to send you a message. It might be the Mob, or it could be someone playing a sick joke. Either way, we have to get you out of Snow Sky."

"Thanks, Verdie. I know this is confusing but I just need some time away. I'll call you in a few days and let you know when to reopen the café." Eloise hung up the phone then turned to Jackson, marveling at how calm she felt now that an hour had passed and she'd gotten over the initial shock of seeing those roses. "Verdie is okay with closing the café for a few days. She's just going in tomorrow to clean up and make sure everything we've already prepared is put away or tossed out. I explained about the break-in but told her not to mention that to anyone. So she truly believes I need a break and time to grieve. What now?"

He gave her that hard stare she was becoming accustomed to. "We leave tonight as planned. It's too risky here for you right now. And until we find out who tried to break into your house, it's going to stay that way."

The power was back on now. Someone had shut off the source at the circuit box on the side of the condo. And the alarm had been reset. But Eloise didn't feel safe here anymore.

"I'll get some things together," she replied. "Can I stay in touch with Verdie?"

"We'll take that day by day. Maybe, just so she doesn't get concerned about you and alert the locals."

He turned to Roark, said something in his ear then nodded. The agent left without a word.

Because she was giving him what she hoped passed for one of his own questioning scowls, Jackson said, "I sent Roark to give Verdie my cell-phone number—don't worry, he'll tell her he's just working on the Meredith Parker case and if she sees or hears anything to call that number. And he'll explain the need for discretion."

Not so sure Verdie would go for that, Eloise didn't have any choice. She might not ever come back here anyway, so what did it matter now. Thinking of her quaint little bakery and café and how hard she'd worked to get it up and going a few years ago only made her want to curl up in a fetal position and never leave her bed. But she had to keep moving, her only thoughts toward the goal of seeing her daughter again.

"Hey," Jackson said, his acute gaze scanning her face, "we're going to fix this."

"Some things can't be fixed," she replied, her hand touching her scar. Then she turned and headed upstairs where Thea was waiting to help her pack a bag.

A little while later, Eloise sat in the back of the dark SUV, Jackson on one side and Duff on the other. Roark drove and Thea sat in the seat across from him. GQ was following in another car.

The dark-tinted windows made the night so black, Eloise could barely see the shapes of the trees and buildings. "I don't like the dark," she said, looking over at Jackson.

"Would someone know that about you?" he asked, ever the agent.

"I did mention it to Verdie and Frank, maybe Meredith."

"And Meredith could have mentioned it to her husband, which might explain the power going off tonight."

"Possibly. Or Randall Parker could have shut down everything so he could get in without anyone seeing him."

"Maybe. I can't see a Chicago capo trying to climb that slim rope to your bedroom window. That does sound more like Parker's MO."

"But the white roses are standard Martino style."

"Did you ever mention that to anyone—that you didn't like white roses?"

"I don't think so. I try to never give any hints of my past life." Did she mention the roses to Meredith? Eloise racked her brain, but couldn't recall doing so.

"Thea will find a link to the roses and when she does, it'll be part of the evidence we'll use against Martino. If Martino deliberately sent the roses, then our leak is getting bolder and so is he."

She nodded. "Thanks for letting me call Verdie."

"You're welcome. Do you think she bought your story?"

Eloise looked down at her hands. "I think so. She's pretty upset herself and she seemed relieved to have a few days off. Besides, she's worried about this murder—worried for my safety and hers. Frank's not leaving her side, either. No word on the funeral yet."

"Autopsies take time."

"When will we know for sure…how Meredith died?"

"You'll know as soon as I do."

That was Jackson-speak for "You'll know when I think you need to know."

He'd always been a stickler for the rules. Eloise remembered how careful he'd been when he was assigned to be her bodyguard so long ago. They'd spent hours together, at first just sitting quietly, then slowly getting to know each other with small talk and later, lots of intimate talks about what they wanted out of life.

"I want to be the best agent I can be," he'd told her. Because his father, a Chicago cop, had died in the line of duty. And his young brother, a preschooler back then, had been on his mind. "Already, Micah wants to be a cop. Already."

She'd seen the worry in Jackson's crystalline eyes. She'd seen that same worry when he looked at her, then and now.

"How's your brother these days?" she asked, because she needed to hear his voice, needed to know what he was thinking.

"Micah? He's okay. We've had our differences. I tried too hard to control him when he was growing up. He thinks I resented him wanting to be a cop, so he moved as far away from me as possible."

"To become a U.S. Marshal in Montana?"

"Yeah, what are the odds?"

She smiled at the familiar phrase they'd used back and forth. It seemed to be the only phrase Jackson offered for any type of personal explanations. "He had no way of knowing—"

"About us? About what happened back then? No, not at first. I only gave him the facts of the case, nothing more."

She let the "about us" slip by. "So he's in a very dangerous business in spite of your concerns and now, he's trying to chase down the family that wants me dead."

"He is, but Micah is one of the best. I need to tell him that one day."

She didn't ask but it was obvious there was something not quite right between Jackson and his brother. If he had indeed tried to protect Micah the way he did everyone else he cared about, she could imagine the young brother felt smothered at times. It was sweet but predictable between two warriors, she supposed. "Do you talk to him a lot?"

"Lately, yes, almost on a daily basis. He's engaged now. Met her on this case."

"And he's helping with this case?"

"He is."

"But you can't tell me anything more, right?"

"Right. Best you don't know."

She had to wonder what *was* best for her at this point. Running again in the dark? Was that the best way to handle this? Hiding in a mountain retreat? Was that courageous or a cop-out? In spite of two dangerous forces chasing her, Eloise didn't understand why after all these years she was once again on the run; she couldn't find the answers she sought, couldn't reason why her simple, uncomplicated life in Snow Sky had become chaotic and uncertain. So she closed her eyes to pray, but the lull of sleep and the steady rocking of the big SUV made her drowsy. And soon the darkness she often feared became a protective cloak around her, causing her to shift in the seat.

And in her slumber, she felt a pair of strong arms cuddling her there in the darkness. And for just a little while, she wasn't so afraid of the black night.

SIX

Jackson couldn't sleep.

The safe house was big and rambling, all cedar and rock, with a beamed A-framed ceiling in the hearth room and a nice country kitchen beyond. The open floor plan and floor-to-ceiling windows on one wall suited his need to have a bird's-eye view of his surroundings while the tinted weatherproof windows didn't allow anyone from the outside to have a clear view inside.

Now, he stood on the upstairs landing where a loft bedroom/den combination was nestled against the back wall. He'd taken this particular room because he could see the whole downstairs from this vantage point. There were two large, private bedroom suites on either side of the loft. Eloise and Thea were in one and Marcus and Roark were in the other.

Duff had decided to stay out here with Jackson.

"You and me, we get each other, don't we, boy?" Jackson said to the faithful dog sitting right at his feet. He leaned down to scratch between Duff's ears and was rewarded with a satisfied doggy sigh. "You'll help me keep her safe, right?"

Duff gave a little woof in agreement.

"Good boy."

Jackson traced back over the last two days, thinking he hadn't had a moment to wind down. But then, he couldn't wind down until they'd captured Martino for good. So he did what he always did when he couldn't sleep. He thought about the case. And this one had turned into a triple threat.

There was a leak in the U.S. Marshal's office—Micah and his team were on that.

There was an informant who refused to show her face and even though Jackson grudgingly accepted that, he also figured she was connected to someone very close to Vincent Martino. Had to be an inside man feeding her with information. Jackson has his own theories on that one, but for now he'd have to let that slide.

Because a Mafia kingpin was out to kill Eloise in some kind of twisted homage to his now-dead father—Jackson was on that one. It would remain a top priority.

And…a bad cop might have murdered his own wife and he might know that Eloise had seen him do it.

What to do about that one?

Jackson did one more visual of the big room below, his eyes trained to the darkness. The glow of yellow security lights out on the deck and below in the big sloping yard gave him some assurance. There really wasn't such a thing as a safe house, but the term came close in this case. They were about as secure and secluded as they could be for now.

And Eloise was safe.

He turned from the log-hewn banister and sat back

down in the high-backed leather chair tucked in a corner along with a small desk. His laptop hummed and glowed so he went back over the files Micah had sent to him through a secure network.

His brother had narrowed down the list of suspects to only a couple now—people who might have access to any and all information filtering through the Marshal's office. And one of them jumped out at Jackson.

Mac Sellers.

Jackson didn't know the man, but the report Micah had sent indicated that Sellers was privy to some very sensitive information, including the names of women matching Eloise's description who'd been brought to Montana through the Witness Protection Program. That alone, however, didn't make the man a suspect since a lot of people would have access to that information anyway.

But the other information Micah had sent sure did. Sellers, once a field agent, had been relegated to a desk job because of an injury that left him walking with a limp. And according to Micah, the man made no bones about how much he hated having to work as a technical investigator, doing research online and in the office, instead of out in the field where the real action always was.

Everyone tends to steer clear of his rants, Micah wrote. *Mainly because he's so good at his job and he's also good at keeping secrets. He gets highly offended whenever anyone questions him about guarded information. It's like he's protesting too much, know what I mean?*

Micah hadn't thought about Sellers until recently, when the man pitched a fit after Micah questioned a file Sellers had pulled—the latest report on the Martino case and several women listed in the Witness Protection Program. Why would Sellers pull that particular file? The man had access to all the information and surely had seen it before. When Micah questioned him, Sellers got defensive. Claimed he was just rechecking some facts. Trying to piece together information to help solve this case, trying to help since no one could put a finger on how this mess got started in the first place.

All well and good, but this file was top secret. Only the task force members Jackson had put in place with Micah had access to this information. So why did Sellers have the file?

That had sent up a red flag.

And that meant they needed to zoom in on Sellers.

But they couldn't accuse the man or alert him to what they suspected. Micah had played it cool with Sellers, telling him he appreciated the double check and asking him to put together his own report on their findings. Was the man pulling information he'd already given to Martino? And if so, why? He called his brother. Micah picked up on the first ring.

"We need to set up a sting," Jackson said. "You take care of that, Micah. Use the task force you have there and bring in other agents if you need to."

"You trust me to do that?"

"Of course I trust you. Why wouldn't I?"

He heard the hesitation, the doubt in his brother's words. "Well, you haven't in the past."

"Micah, we're in this together. We'll finish it together. Yes, I trust you. I know you'll find the leak."

"How?" Micah amended that. "I mean, where do you want me to start?"

Jackson, used to issuing orders, had refrained. "You tell me."

"Make sure Sellers has access to a phony report on one of the women. List her as a priority and 'move' her to a location that Sellers will be sure to hear about."

"That's a good plan."

Micah finished up, "And if anyone from Martino's organization happens to show up in that location, then we can bet Sellers is our leak, right?"

"Right. Especially if you make sure he gets the information directly, but in a normal way, so as not to alert him."

After they agreed to which name to use and how they'd get a decoy agent to play the part of a WWP woman, Micah hung up, promising to go into action and to keep Jackson posted.

If they could stop this leak, that would be one burden off Jackson's shoulders—and a big feather in Micah's cap, too. If Sellers was their man, they'd make him talk and hopefully give them the goods on Martino.

And find out why he'd felt it necessary to get even for his accident by helping the Mafia kill innocent women.

Most likely, money had played a part in the informant's need to side with the Martino family. Lots of Mafia money. Dirty money, Jackson thought now.

He heard a door opening down the hall and automatically shut down the laptop.

Duff lifted up to greet Eloise as she walked into the loft area wearing a fluffy blue robe and cotton pajamas.

She glanced around, saw Jackson sitting there with a single table lamp burning then frowned. "Don't you ever sleep?"

"I get by. What's your excuse?"

She shot him a sleepy frown. "Do I really need to explain that?"

"No, I guess not." He took in the sight of her. Her long dark hair fell in chocolate-velvet ribbons around her face and neck. She held her hands wrapped against her waist, a defensive gesture that he'd seen her use a lot. Her eyes, devoid of the colored contacts, were so dark they reminded him of a lush green forest.

"But you—you get by?" She lifted off the beam she'd been perched against. "Is that any way to live, Jackson?"

"It's my way."

Eloise walked to the desk then turned, her hands clutching the heavy banister. She looked down at the dying fire in the stone fireplace below. "When was the last time you had a decent meal?"

Thinking that was an odd question to ask at 2:00 a.m., Jackson shrugged. "We all had burgers in the car, remember?"

"C'mon," she said, reaching out for his hand.

Shocked, Jackson let her fingers settle against his skin. Her hand felt small in his, but she had surprising strength, a strength that allowed her to halfway pull him out of his chair and tug him down the big stairs toward the kitchen, Duff on their heels.

"Eloise, you need to rest."

"I can't sleep, either. And when I can't sleep, I cook," she said. "And you look like an omelet man."

Jackson's mouth watered. Glad Thea had made sure the kitchen was stocked, he smiled. "I remember omelets—eggs, ham, peppers, onions." He hadn't realized he was starving until he watched her go about finding everything she needed to fix him a meal.

But he wasn't starving for food.

He'd been starving for something much more substantial and lasting—the sight of seeing her in a big, beautiful kitchen with a smile on her face as she cooked…for him.

"And coffee," she said, swinging around to find the coffeepot. "I know you like coffee since it's the only beverage I've seen you drink. You might want to add orange juice and water to your list of beverages. They're good for you."

"Yes, ma'am." He grinned, and his facial muscles groaned at this unusual stretch. He couldn't remember the last time he'd really grinned. How sad was that?

Soon the smell of ham mixed with peppers and onions permeated the air.

"You'll have the whole gang down here, wanting to eat," he told her.

"I can feed them as a way to thank them," she replied. "But Thea was snoring the cutest little snore when I snuck out."

He had to laugh at that. "Thea snores?"

"She does, but it's sweet, not annoying. She's a nice kid."

"She's a highly trained agent."

That brought some levity back to the night. "Well, let her sleep. She deserves it. And you deserve a good meal."

Jackson leaned forward, basking in the swirl of long-dormant feelings warming up his soul. "You know, Kristin can't cook."

Eloise stopped, an egg held in midair. "Not a bit?"

"Really." He drummed his fingers on the tile of the big counter. "Her adoptive mother wasn't as motivated about cooking and baking as you are."

Eloise broke the egg into the bowl with the others she'd already put in and started beating them, her eyes on Jackson. "I don't think a knack for baking can be inherited, but it's good to know anyway. I want to know everything about her. I need to know—"

"And I'll tell you anything. We have lots of time."

She stopped, dropping the wooden spoon against the big glass bowl. "Do we…have lots of time?"

Jackson could see the doubt and fear in her eyes. How could he promise her something he couldn't be sure of? "We will," he said, meaning it. He'd make sure of it, somehow. "You'll get to see your daughter again, Ellie."

"It's too much to hope for," she said. Then she went about the business of cooking his omelet, her gaze intent on the work at hand while she stewed in her own thoughts.

The kitchen grew quiet except for the sizzle of the eggs bubbling against the frying pan and the drip of the coffeepot finishing up the brew.

Jackson's brief flash of contentment was gone, to be replaced with a helplessness that pulled at him, making him heavy with fatigue. Maybe it was too much to hope for, this wanting, this need to keep her safe. Maybe it was too much to hope for, seeing her again and remembering the sweet tenderness of that young love, that first love—it had never left him. He'd held those memories close and hidden in a secret place and he'd tried so hard not to pull them out, not to look at them.

But the memories couldn't compare to this night, right here, right now. Eloise cooking for him, smiling at him, laughing with him. Ellie, safe and in his sights.

"Jackson?"

He looked up to find her standing across from him, a perfect creamy-yellow omelet centered on a big plate with a sprig of parsley, buttered toast and a sliced orange gracing it.

"Your food is ready." She set the plate in front of him and placed a steaming cup of coffee beside it. "Eat."

Jackson stared at the plate of food, starving.

Then he looked up at her, got up and came around the counter to pull her into his arms, his hands tugging at her hair, his lips touching hers, with joy, with sorrow and with promise. This reunion was risky, he knew. This kiss was dangerous, he knew.

But he also knew that some things were worth the risk and the danger. And kissing Eloise again was worth everything that had brought him to this moment.

Upstairs, a door opened then shut, but Jackson didn't care who may have seen them. His agents could be discreet. And he'd stare them down to make sure.

He lifted his head, looked down into her big, frightened eyes and kissed her on the nose. "Thank you. I'm starving."

Then he turned and sat back down and ate his first decent meal in months.

While she stood there, half in shock, half smiling, and watched him.

Eloise woke up to sun shining through the sheers on the double balcony doors of the big master bedroom. Thea wasn't anywhere in the room and the bathroom door stood open. Eloise was alone.

She stretched then settled back against the pillows to take in the tree line just beyond the wide upstairs balcony. She'd slept, at last. Slept late, too, from the tilt of the sun's rays falling across the quilted cover on the big bed.

Jackson had kissed her. A solid, demanding, good kiss.

A mature and confident kiss—something she dreamed of long ago. Just a kiss.

Then he'd eaten like a man who hadn't had food in days, which was probably true, and they'd talked and talked, about everything: Kristin; his job—the parts he could talk about; his brother, Micah, and how proud Jackson was of him; about Micah's new love, Jade, and about anything and everything but the obvious—Martino and this death threat; Randall Parker and Meredith's death and all the things holding Eloise and Jackson apart. They'd only talked like normal people.

Normal. What was normal?

She sat up, closed her eyes and thanked God for another day. And Jackson. "Thank you, Lord, for sending him to me. Thank you for protecting my daughter, Kristin. Keep her safe. Keep Jackson safe. Help me to find a way out of this, Lord."

She opened her eyes and relived Jackson's kiss all over. It made her smile even while it scared her, thinking about the intensity of that kiss. She knew she could easily fall for Jackson again.

"Again?" she said on a whisper. "Again? How about this, Ellie? How about you never got over him to begin with?"

She was still in love with Jackson McGraw.

And that admission put a solid fear in her heart. What if he died trying to protect her? What then?

Eloise prayed that wouldn't happen. Surely God hadn't brought Jackson back into her life so she'd wind up losing him again? *Please, Lord, watch over him. He's a good man and he's seen too much pain and sorrow. We both have.*

With her prayers front and center in her mind, she took a quick shower and threw on a black turtleneck sweater and matching black knit pants. After putting on some blush and lip gloss, she hurried down the wide, open staircase.

And stopped at the sound of Jackson's orders to his team.

"This means Martino was in Snow Sky this morning,

Roark. We don't need this, and we certainly don't need Parker making open appeals on the local television station for Eloise to step forward."

"What?" Eloise asked as she moved down the stairs. "What are you talking about?"

Jackson turned, his hands on his hips, his scowl etching deep wrinkles around his eyes. Back to being the agent in charge, he stared up at her. "Verdie was attacked this morning in the café."

Eloise gasped. "What? Is she all right? Should I go to her?"

He held up a hand. "She's fine. The paramedics took her to the hospital just to be sure. She called the number I left with her, because she was worried the same thing might happen to you."

"How?" Eloise came down into the hearth room and sank on the long leather couch. "How, Jackson?"

He let out a sigh. "She'd gone in to clean up and make sure the place was shut down. Two men—she described them as big and burly and wearing black overcoats—came into the café. Pushed their way in, according to Verdie. Frank had gone to the bank to make a deposit and she was there by herself, clearing out the counters. Anyway, they asked a lot of questions about you. When she got suspicious and reached for the phone, one of the men pushed her backward and she hit her head on the stove as she fell. Frank found her lying there and the men got away."

"Martino's men?" Eloise asked, her heart stopped, her breath caught in her throat.

"Probably, ma'am," Thea said. "We can't compare notes with the locals—it would blow our cover."

"But Verdie was attacked. Why can't one of you go back over there and help her?"

"I'll put somebody on it," Jackson said. "But not this team. I need them here, Ellie."

"For me? You need them to protect me while my friends are being murdered and attacked. Jackson, just let me go to the police in Snow Sky and tell them what I saw. At least let me get that off my conscience."

"You can't," he said, shaking his head. "Detective Parker has gone on the local news and announced that you're missing, that you left town. And he needs to question you about his wife's murder." He stepped toward her then leaned over the arm of the sofa. "Ellie, he's plastered your picture all over the news stations and in the papers. Martino's thugs obviously know you live there, but this will verify things for them."

Eloise shook her head. "No, I can't believe this. Why is Randall Parker doing that?"

"He apparently thinks you know something about his wife's death," Roark explained. "As in—maybe you had something to do with it."

"He's blaming me?" she asked, bolting up to pace the floor. "Jackson, he's trying to pin this on me?"

"It looks that way. He just said you're wanted for questioning and that you're a 'person of interest.' He implied you had a very strong influence over his wife." He grabbed her arms to still her. "It's his way of threatening you. He thinks if you come into the station, he can get to you first and save his own hide." He let out another breath. "That…or he's figured out you saw him that night and he's setting a trap for you. Either way, you won't be going back to Snow Sky. But Marcus is going over there and he's going to explain to the locals in no uncertain terms that you're in danger and they'd better back off—"

"But what about the cover?"

"Marcus will explain about that, too. He's going straight to the captain—official FBI business and on a need-to-know basis."

"It won't work. They'll protect Parker, not me. He's got all of them convinced he's perfect."

Marcus stepped forward. "I don't think so, Ms. Smith. Parker and the captain—not so good. We managed to pull some old newspaper reports and some 'unofficial' reports on the locals in Snow Sky. Parker has it in for Captain Lewis and from what we can gather—the feeling is mutual."

Jackson looked at her, his hands softening on her arms. "You can't go back there, Ellie. It's just not safe. And Parker needs to shut up."

She pulled away. "Well, good luck with making that happen."

Then she stomped out the front door, the morning wind hitting her even as the sun's warmth shot down on her.

Such beauty, all around her. The mountains bloomed with the colors of summer, bitterroot and buttercups bright with pinks and yellows, Aspen trees and Indian paintbrush rimming the stream and orchard below the cabin. The birds chirped and fussed, the trees rustled with a playful wind. She could hear the falls off in the distance as they danced down the rock bed. Reminding herself that the bitterroot was called the resurrection flower because it could break through dry ground to grow again, she wondered if she could find that same kind of strength.

But the beauty couldn't replace the fear Eloise felt deep inside her bones. In spite of the beautiful morning and the pretty pink flowers that had come back from a winter death, the dread inside her heart felt as cold as winter and each sound and sigh of this mountain became an unrelenting threat. And it was a threat that even a kiss and a promise, and the hope of finding love again, couldn't overcome.

SEVEN

Jackson waited until the man he'd been watching reached the door of the second-floor apartment. Then he moved in.

"Detective Randall Parker?"

Randall Parker whirled, the open door to his apartment slapping against the wall behind him. "Yeah?"

Jackson sized up the man. Handsome and rugged, a real bad-boy type with dark blond hair and cruel hazel eyes. He stared Jackson down, defiant and with a cool disregard.

"Whoever you are, I'm not interested," Parker said, turning to head into the apartment.

Jackson followed, blocking the door with a booted foot when the detective tried to shut it in his face. "We need to talk," Jackson said, flashing his badge.

Parker looked doubtful at first but Jackson caught the quick panic in his eyes. "A fed from Chicago? What's this about?"

Jackson pushed him into the room and slammed the door shut. "This, Detective, is about Ellie Smith."

Parker's panicked look turned to sick dread. "Hey, man, I just want to talk to the woman. What'd she do, call in the big dogs?" He shrugged. "You're out of your jurisdiction, aren't you?"

Jackson grabbed the lapels of Parker's leather jacket. He had to make this believable or Parker would get suspicious. "You need to back off, understand? Ellie Smith doesn't know anything about your wife's death and it's really not a good thing—you putting her name and picture out there for all to see."

Parker lifted away, then shook his head, his panic gone now as he looked Jackson over with an intense suspicion. "What's she got to hide? And what's this got to do with the FBI?" He hit a hand on the wall. "Hey, was that you feds prowling around her yard the other night?"

Jackson pretended indifference. "Were *you* prowling around her house?"

"Maybe," Parker said, his expression turning wary. "Who wants to know?"

"I do," Jackson replied. "You're messing in something you don't need to be messing in, Detective Parker."

"Yeah, well, I'm trying to find out something about my dead wife, okay?"

"And you think Ellie Smith can help with that?"

"Yeah, since I'm pretty sure she was trying to get my wife to leave me. I think she knows something."

Jackson wanted to ask the detective more about that, but he refrained. "Well, we need to talk to Ellie Smith ourselves and you're getting in the way."

"So you do have something on her?"

"We almost had that figured out until you scared her off," Jackson said, letting Parker go. "But we might not find out anything if you keep mouthing off to the media." He didn't say anything else, hoping Parker would fill in the blanks.

And he did.

Doing a little spin, the detective whirled back to face Jackson. "Are you telling me the FBI is investigating Ellie Smith?"

Jackson lifted a brow but remained quiet.

This had been a risky decision, one Roark and Marcus had advised against. But he'd take the blame for it if anything came up. Right now, Roark was talking to Captain Lewis and Jackson was here to distract Detective Parker and hopefully scare him silly while he was at it. He had to imply they were investigating Ellie or the savvy detective would bolt. He just prayed Parker would fall for it and keep his mouth shut for a while.

When Jackson neither denied nor agreed with him, Parker let out a whistle. "Man, I can't believe this. I always knew there was something not right with that woman. She was always so quiet and so private about where she came from. And then when she started buddying up with Meredith, well… But I never could find any dirt on her. Hey, if you need me to dig deeper, I can do that. I mean, I've tried but so far…nothing solid. She's a do-gooder, you know. Goes to church and donates food to the local homeless shelter, things so squeaky-clean it makes you want to throw up." He stopped, then leaned close. "I'd be glad to get something on that woman."

"Thanks, but we've got it." Jackson breathed a sigh

of relief even while he itched to slug the man. This self-centered murderer had fallen for the bait, and because his ego couldn't let him see beyond the trap he'd just stepped into, he was more than willing to spill his guts. "You can do us a big favor and back off for a while. We need to continue our investigation, but if you keep exposing her she'll leave Snow Sky for good. And then we all lose. So…can you keep quiet for a while longer so maybe she'll come back and we can continue this case?"

Parker looked doubtful then pushed a hand through his hair. "Yeah, sure. I just want to ask her about Meredith. I think those two were cooking something up. I just need to know what she knows, so I can find my wife's murderer." He took a long breath, his torn expression begging for sympathy while he rubbed his chin. "Do you know her current location? If I could just talk to her—"

"We think we know," Jackson replied, his gut telling him the man was lying about his reasons for wanting to see Eloise. He was overexplaining himself and his body language indicated he was very uncomfortable. "Sorry, I can't tell you for sure where Ms. Smith is—she's gone underground apparently."

"Because she obviously has something to hide." Parker nodded then walked around the counter of the tiny efficiency kitchen just off the entryway, his keys jingling in his hand. "I'd be willing to cooperate a little more if I knew the situation."

Jackson didn't like this man but he played along. "You first. What have you got so far?"

"Um, like I said, not much. Nobody's talking and Miss High-and-Mighty wouldn't show her face after I…uh, after we found Meredith dead. I went to her house and tried to talk to her, but she wouldn't open the door, you know. And that infernal dog is always hanging around—never understood why she takes that mongrel everywhere. That makes me believe she knows something and that's why I went to the television station." He picked up a salt shaker then slid it across the counter.

Fidgety, Jackson noted. Nervous, stalling and practically stuttering over his words, putting a barrier between them. The man was lying about everything.

"Did you happen to see her actually leaving her place?"

Parker shook his head. "I watched her apartment for a while, hoping just to speak to her. But my captain put me on another case. That man is always riding me—said I wasn't in any shape to handle this." He shrugged then looked down. "Once I had some free time, I found out from that teenage squirt at the café that Smith had left town."

Jackson nodded, pretending to commiserate with the detective. "Could be trouble, trying to flush her out like that. Do you have reason to believe Ms. Smith did your wife some sort of harm?"

Detective Parker immediately became even more evasive. If the man didn't quit shrugging, he was going to get a serious neck spasm. "Um, look, man, like I said, I don't know what's going on with her. I just know she was way too involved in my wife's personal business and um…I'm guessing she knows what was going on with Meredith the night she died."

The look in his eyes begged Jackson to contradict him. So he was worried about *someone* seeing what had happened that night. And he was trying to guess how much Jackson knew.

"Did she give you some trouble?"

"I got enough trouble," Parker countered, "without that woman interfering." Throwing his keys down on the counter, he said, "But I'd sure like to know what the feds have on our dear little Ellie."

"Sorry, like I said, I can't talk about an active case," Jackson replied with a studied smile. "We'd appreciate your cooperation though. If you keep *this* just between you and me, we could maybe keep *you* in the loop. Unofficially. I mean, I know you want to find your wife's killer."

Parker's eyes sparked with interest, his pupils dilating with glee. "Sure, and maybe y'all could pass on anything you find to me in return? You know, a favor for a favor?"

Jackson figured this man called in favors all the time, one way or another. "I'll see what I can do. But only if you drop the rants to the media. You've already made the woman bolt. She might not ever come back."

Parker rubbed his hands together. "I'd sure like to know what you've got on her."

Jackson stared him down but didn't respond. He had to give the man points for persistence, though.

"Oh, right. Can't talk about it."

"And we need to keep this on the down-low," Jackson

reminded him. "I'm serious on that. You keep going with your investigation and we'll keep things together on ours. Without bringing in our superiors."

Parker looked unsure but nodded. "Whatever you say. But I would like to compare notes."

Jackson handed the man a card. "Here's my personal number. Call me if you hear or see anything."

Parker took the card. "So you really don't know where she is?"

"Nope. And thanks to you, we might not ever find her."

Parker didn't seem too concerned. "I have ways of finding people." He winked. "And most of them aren't too happy when they see me coming."

"I can only imagine," Jackson said with a fake smile. He wanted to throttle the smug man but he reminded himself he had to play this cool for Ellie's sake. "But like I said, we'll handle it from here on out. But keep in touch."

Parker shot him one more scrutinizing look. "You know I'll have to verify everything you just told me."

Jackson had been expecting that. "I wouldn't have it any other way. Call Washington, D.C., if you need to. I can assure you my credentials are legitimate. And so is this case. But you might keep in mind that any attention you bring to yourself could jeopardize your chances of finding your wife's killer. Or force us to dig into your past, too."

That much was the truth at least. Jackson hoped the detective took it as the threat it implied.

That statement seemed to do the trick with the

detective. "Good point. I'll just keep investigating on the side. If my captain knew this, he'd have my hide. That man and me—we don't see eye to eye."

"I get that a lot, too," Jackson said. He made one last sweep of the small room. And his gaze landed on a backpack and bundle of rope lying by the old sofa.

Rope that looked a lot like the rope they'd found at Eloise's place.

Jackson lifted his gaze back to Parker.

Parker glanced at the rope then back to Jackson.

They seemed to communicate with a silence that stretched as firm and taut as that bright rope.

Parker had been the one trying to break into Eloise's house the other night. Jackson's gut told him that much at least. But had the detective brought the roses, too?

"You do some climbing?" Jackson asked, his voice as calm as a still lake.

Parker chuckled, still fidgeting while he stayed trapped behind the counter. "When I have time, yeah. But doesn't everybody around here?"

"I wouldn't know," Jackson replied, turning for the door. "We don't climb mountains in Chicago."

"But you do chase bad guys, or in this case, a bad woman?"

Jackson didn't answer. He didn't have to. He'd seen enough to know Parker was probably onto Eloise. Parker had to know that she'd been the figure up on the landing that night, hidden in the shadows. And that verified all of Eloise's fears. And Jackson's worries.

And now, Parker had probably figured the FBI might

be watching him, too. Maybe the not knowing would be enough to give Jackson some time.

Or maybe not.

She was worried.

Eloise didn't know why she missed Jackson so much. She had Thea for immediate company and Roark was standing watch outside. Or rather, he was sitting in a rocking chair, pretending to be reading a book. But Eloise had learned these agents could be deceptive when they were doing their job. Thea, pretending to be focused on a crossword puzzle; Roark, intent on reading the latest mystery-thriller. They were on high alert and they were protecting her.

Even Duff seemed to be picking up FBI tactics. He looked sleepy as he lay by her feet, but every now and then the dog would lift his head, his eyes going up at the slightest sound.

Maybe Duff missed Jackson, too.

Thinking about how Jackson had kissed her last night, Eloise couldn't help but wonder if they had any chance of a future together. *Not now,* she thought. *Not when I have so much hanging over my head.*

It was just a kiss, nothing more. A moment to treasure and remember when she was alone and afraid and not so sure of her future. Just a kiss. Followed by the whispered, "I'm starving."

Eloise knew that kind of hunger—the hunger for love, the hunger for safety and security, the need to know and feel another human being's concern and closeness.

Dear God, I know how he feels. Please, dear Lord, help us both to be filled with Your grace and mercy. Help us to find our way.

The oven timer dinged and Eloise got up to take out the bread she'd baked earlier. Apple cheddar with chopped walnuts.

"That smells so good," Thea said, getting up to follow Eloise into the kitchen. Another move that seemed perfectly normal but was meant as a bodyguard tactic. Jackson had left strict instructions that Eloise was not to be left alone in any room in the house. So even though this was a big, open room, Thea felt obligated to hover close.

"We'll make some coffee and cut a few slices," Eloise said, grinning.

"Cooking seems to keep you calm," Thea noted, smiling back. "Me, I manage to burn a frozen microwave meal."

Eloise shook her head. "It seems to me that FBI agents don't eat right."

"We're too busy getting the job done," Thea admitted. "I love those assignments where the cover involves going to restaurants. Though we usually have to leave our food steaming on the table if the subjects get up and leave."

"Not a good way to live," Eloise countered.

"No, but it's part of the job. And we all believe in what we do."

Eloise saw the sincerity in Thea's dark eyes. "Jackson speaks highly of all of you."

"He speaks highly of you, too, ma'am."

Unable to resist, Eloise asked, "Does he…talk about me a lot?"

"Not really," Thea replied, realization at her slip dawning in her eyes. "He's so focused on finding Martino, he eats, sleeps and breathes that."

"You can't tell me, can you?"

Thea glanced around then leaned close. "I can tell you this. He cares a lot about you and your daughter. This case has been like a bad ache for him—for months now. When he put this team together, he made us vow to do our jobs, keep our mouths shut and…get Martino. And he warned us it would be one of the most dangerous assignments we'd ever had."

Eloise shuddered, crossing her arms tightly against her chest. "Martino is very dangerous. I'm so sorry Jackson can't seem to shake this."

Thea stood up straight. "He will, ma'am. He will. He won't give up until he's done just that."

Duff got up and rushed to the door, his tail wagging.

Eloise looked up to find Jackson standing there, his eyes centered on her.

Thea looked guilty as she averted her eyes.

"You two having a heart-to-heart?" Jackson asked, his gaze scanning Eloise's face.

"Isn't that what two women with time on their hands do?" Eloise asked. Then she pointed toward the sliced bread. "Hungry?"

Jackson didn't take his gaze off her. "Starving."

Thea glanced from Jackson to Eloise and Eloise was sure the girl could see her blush.

Thea grabbed two slices of bread and headed toward the double doors onto the deck. "I'm sure Roark will appreciate this, ma'am."

Jackson stood staring at Eloise.

"Where have you been?" she asked. "Did you find out anything else about Parker or the two men who attacked Verdie?"

He didn't answer. He strolled over to the kitchen then broke off a hunk of apple cheddar bread. Biting into it, he finally spoke. "I found out enough."

"And?"

"And, that's for me to worry about."

Eloise knew he wouldn't tell her anything else.

But his eyes said it all. Parker was still a threat to her. And that meant Jackson's burden had not been lightened.

Eloise thought about running again. She could take off in the middle of the night. She could start over. She'd done it before. She knew how to be careful. How to disappear.

Jackson dropped the bread and came around the counter.

"Don't even think it," he said, his face inches from hers.

"You don't know what I'm thinking," she replied, wishing she could take away his pain.

"Oh, yes, I'm pretty sure I do. I didn't see it all those years ago because I was…distracted. But this time, Eloise, I'm focused. On saving you. And if you run again, I won't have that chance."

"Is that what this is about, Jackson? Having a

second chance to wipe away what you consider your one mistake?"

"Yes," he said, bobbing his head, his eyes wide, his frown pulled by anger. "Yes, Ellie. I made *a lot* of mistakes and if I can fix just one—"

"If you can get Martino and save my life, you'll be absolved?"

"I'll never be absolved," he shot back. "But at least I can sleep better at night, knowing I got it right this time."

"And that's the only reason you're here, forcing me to go into hiding? Just so you can sleep better."

He reached for her then backed away, his expression grim, his eyes hard. But his words almost broke her with their honesty and sweetness. "That and…just knowing you're safe and alive. I can live with that."

Eloise didn't know how to respond. He was willing to do anything to keep her alive. Even if it meant he'd have to give her up a second time to make that happen.

"I won't run, Jackson. I'm tired of running. But I won't stand around and watch you put yourself on the line just to prove a point, either."

"What are you saying?"

"I'm saying that you need to take care of yourself. You do need to stay focused. And you need to remember that I'd like to see *you* safe and alive, too." She moved toward him, getting into his space the way he'd done with her. "Don't sacrifice yourself for me, okay? I couldn't live with that."

Before he could form a retort, the door opened then slammed with a pop. "I think we've got company,

Jackson," Roark said, binoculars in his hand. "I picked up a car moving at a fast speed up the road toward the house. And it's not GQ."

"Did he report in?"

"No, not in the last hour," Roark shouted. "I'll try to locate him."

Jackson's gaze slammed into Eloise's for just a split second. And then everyone went into action, and in spite of being dragged away from the windows, she was lost in that split second.

Because in that brief glimpse, she'd seen everything right there in his eyes.

He loved her.

And she loved him.

And that realization terrified her more than Vincent Martino ever could. Because it meant she had yet another reason to live.

And Jackson had a reason to die.

EIGHT

"Roark, talk to me."

"Got it, sir. Just the one driver, no passengers that I can tell. Driver's wearing a hat. Can't make an identity." Roark held the binoculars tightly against his brow. "And Marcus isn't answering his phone."

Jackson held Eloise behind him in the far corner of the big, open room. He could slip her out the back at a minute's notice. If whoever this was hadn't already placed people around the entire house. "See anybody else out there?"

"Negative." Roark moved from window to window, scanning the yard and woods. "No one that I can spot. No boats or watercrafts on the lake, either."

Jackson took a breath then leaned toward Eloise. "It could be sightseers or a maintenance person. We're just making sure."

She nodded, her eyes wide as she glanced back up at him. "I hate this, Jackson."

"You and me both."

Roark and Thea stalked from window to window. "Nothing," Thea shouted back. "The car's pulling up to the house."

"Stay cool," Jackson ordered. "Roark—"

"Already on it." Roark drew his weapon and headed toward the front door.

Jackson held Eloise close, so close he could feel her heart thumping against his jacket, beating in unison with his own. "Stay right here and stay behind me," he told her.

Roark waited about two beats then opened the door, his gun drawn and centered on the person on the porch. "Don't come any farther."

"It's me," Marcus called, holding up a hand. He took off the dark cap. "Hey, it's me. Didn't you see me?"

Roark let out a grunt of a sigh. "Well, no. That's not the car you left in this morning and I don't recall you wearing that stupid hat, either."

Jackson felt relief washing over him, then anger. "Marcus? What were you thinking?" he asked at the top of his lungs as he stalked into the middle of the room. "We could have shot you."

Marcus didn't even blink. Instead, he motioned to Duff. "Did the dog alert?"

"No," Roark said, surprised. "He did bark once or twice, but that's about it."

"Well, there you have it," Marcus replied, nodding toward Duff. "Duff knew I was a friend."

"He didn't inform us of that," Roark replied evenly before giving Duff a disappointed look. "And he wasn't the one on watch out on the porch."

"But…he knew," Marcus said. "And in answer to your question, Big Mac, *I was thinking* that since some-one was tailing me when I was leaving Snow Sky, that

I probably should ditch the rental car I was in and find another one. So that's what I did. I left that one in a parking lot, went into a convenience store and ducked out the back, then called a cab to take me to the nearest rental place. And…I got this car, such as it is."

"You should have called ahead," Roark said, his grin not quite happy as he yanked at the sock cap Marcus was holding.

Marcus shrugged. "I was more concerned about who was behind me than what lay ahead of me, man. And…I was a just a tad concerned about radio frequencies and a possible GPS on my cell and my car, if you get my drift. I couldn't risk calling in—my gut said no."

"What makes you think that?" Jackson asked in an impatient tone. If Marcus's gut was talking then Jackson needed to listen.

Marcus waved a hand in the air. "Oh, maybe because when I got back to the original rental car I could tell it'd been tampered with." He shrugged. "I don't know about my phone since it never left my pocket. I just had a feeling. So I decided to come in under the radar."

"Okay, all right," Jackson said, disapproval radiating through his system. "So you're here now and lucky for you, Roark didn't plug you full of bullets. Who do you think was tailing you?"

Marcus patted Duff on the head, eyed the cheddar bread and walked over to grab a big hunk. Taking a bite, he closed his eyes and savored the bread. "Two of 'em. Big, burly and completely out of place. Pretty sure it was Martino's men. Must have spotted me coming out of the police station."

Jackson stared over at him, wondering if he should reprimand the man or give him a medal. "You're sure?"

"Well, they didn't look like tourists. You know, all dark haired and wearing dark shades and overcoats. Overcoats, when it's close to eighty-five degrees out there. Give me a break."

"And you're sure you lost them?"

"Didn't see them when I got in the cab and didn't see them again when I hightailed it out of town in that *plain, ordinary* car." He did a neck roll. "Hey, you know me better than that. Sorry I didn't call. I thought—"

"Don't think," Jackson said. "You know the protocol. You know to stay in communication at all times."

"You're right," Marcus said, turning serious. "But...I had other things on my mind, too, sir. And I had one more very good reason for not communicating with you guys."

Jackson's head came up. Marcus was thorough and always a pro. Maybe he did have a good excuse for scaring the daylights out of all of them. "Oh, and what was that, Agent Powell?"

"I was also being tailed by Detective Randall Parker. At least, I think he was tailing me. To tell you the truth, though, it looked like he was tailing the Martino capos, too."

Jackson's head was going to split wide open. Rubbing his forehead with two fingers, he shifted on his chair and let out a grunt. They were all sitting around the big dining table, trying to figure out what to do next.

Eloise got up, rustled through the pantry, then came back with a glass of water and two pain pills. "Take this," she said, giving him a look that told him he'd better do as she said.

Jackson gulped down the tablets then finished off the water. "Thank you." Then he looked down at the chart he'd put together. "Go ahead and say it. I should have stayed away from Parker." And now Ellie knew.

Marcus shook his head. "I figure he saw us entering Ms. Smith's apartment at some point and he's put things together already. Maybe he fell for your cover story or maybe he was just playing along in hopes of getting information."

"Or maybe I gave him exactly what he needed," Jackson replied, disgust in the words. In spite of vowing to stay focused, he was way too distracted to be heading this task force.

Eloise sat down next to him. "Jackson, he's a smart cop. He's good at his job and if he did watch my house then he knows something. And now, you're pretty sure he tried to break in, too. So he had to know someone was there with me that night. The dog was barking and everyone was running around. He's not stupid. He would have eventually put it all together whether I stayed there or not."

Jackson looked down at the chart. "So we have Parker on one end, trying to get to you and we have Martino's men snooping around, trying to find out information about you. Plus, someone left you roses twice. Had to be the Mob since Parker's wife wasn't dead the first time you received flowers." He glanced around the table.

"But if they compare notes with Parker, then the stakes get even higher."

Thea held up a hand. "What if Parker saw one of the Martino goons trying to leave those roses at the apartment that night?"

Jackson nodded. "And he tailed that person or persons, trying to figure out why they'd want to leave roses so late at night?"

Thea jotted down some notes. "Parker would cover all the bases. He might have thought it strange or maybe his detective instincts kicked in and he decided to investigate."

"But that doesn't mean he knows anything," Marcus said. "Although he apparently knew enough to *make* me and probably those thugs, too."

"Well, Martino's thugs could get tired of being tailed by one of the locals and decide to off Parker the next time they see him," Roark offered up. "That would solve one problem."

"Especially if they think he's onto them," Marcus added. "Maybe we should force the issue, set Parker up."

"We can't do that," Jackson said. "Yes, we're pretty sure he killed his wife and that he tried to break into Ellie's place, but we can't just put the Mafia on the man. Even though I'm tempted, believe me."

"He did kill his wife," Eloise said, her tone firm. "I don't know how the flowers got there, but I know Randall Parker killed Meredith."

"I believe you," Jackson replied. Then he told them about the rope he'd seen in Parker's apartment.

"But that still doesn't prove he was there that night," Thea said. "And we won't know anything until we hear back from the State lab on the rope and grapple hook we found."

"Check on that for me," Jackson said. "And see how Meredith Parker's autopsy is coming along."

She got up. "Yes, sir."

"Marcus, what did you find out from Captain Lewis?"

Marcus took a sip of his diet soda. "Oh, he had lots to say about Detective Parker. Good at his job, bad with people skills. The man's been written up, put on probation and investigated by internal affairs so much he should get a medal for being a bad boy. Excessive force being one of his finer traits."

"Any reports on domestic abuse?" Jackson asked.

"As a matter of fact, the captain had a couple of those on him, too. His wife called in two times in the last two years, but she always dropped the charges. Lewis thinks Parker intimidated her into keeping quiet. They always made up and that was that, according to the captain. And the department put a lid on it. Probably why none of this showed up in the first report we found."

"And how does the captain feel about her death?"

"Not good, sir. Not good at all. He wouldn't elaborate, but he's concerned. He's willing to work with us to that end—to prove or disprove that one of his top detectives did or did not kill his wife. He wants to keep it low-key, however. The big chief favors Parker and lets him slide a lot because he's so good at his job."

"And have we heard anything from Great Falls?

What about the records we want pulled from the first wife's murder?"

"I'll check on that," Roark said, moving away from the table. "Maybe something's come through since I put in the request yesterday."

"Okay," Jackson said, giving a nod. "From what I saw of the detective, he was lying about a lot of things and he's itching to talk to Meredith. He's thinking she saw something and he wants to get to her before anyone else. If he made you today, Marcus, then he's probably thinking you were at the station investigating Eloise, not him. And he followed you, hoping to find her."

"Which he didn't," Marcus said, pleased with himself. "And he won't, sir. As for the Martino goons—I'd say they're stewing away at some Snow Sky hotel, biding their time until they can snoop around some more. Probably bringing more roses, too, just to add that special Mob touch."

"Yes, biding their time until they find out where Eloise is," Jackson added, glancing over at her. "And as long as she's with us and we don't lose our cool, she will be protected. Right?"

"Right, sir," Marcus said, nodding. "Absolutely right." He glanced out toward the woods. "Although I have to wonder how both Parker and Martino's men knew to tail *me*. I mean, there where several people milling around the station. Why follow me in particular?"

Jackson wondered that same thing. "Do you think

someone's tipped Parker off and he just got in line behind the Martino men, trying to tail you?"

Marcus rubbed his chin. "I did meet his partner— tall, skinny man with skittish brown eyes—George Andrews."

Jackson looked at Eloise. "He and another officer came to talk to Eloise the morning Meredith Parker was found. He and Parker would naturally be comparing information." He made a note. "We need to talk to Skinny—somebody get me some information on Parker's partner."

Eloise touched Jackson's arm. "I think I might know a little about that."

Surprised, he stared over at her. "Keep talking."

"Verdie mentioned Marcus again—she saw him that morning in the café, remember?"

"I remember," Jackson replied. "But she has no idea who he is, right?"

Eloise shook her head. "No, but…she did mention that he seemed highly interested in Meredith's death— he was still there when the police came in to tell Verdie about Meredith, remember?"

Jackson glanced at Marcus. "Yeah, but Marcus knows how to stand back and observe." He glared at Marcus. "You did stand back, Agent Powell?"

Marcus bobbed his head. "Yes, sir. I listened and absorbed information. But before the cops came in, I was carrying on a conversation with Verdie—trying to get information."

Eloise glanced between the two of them. "When I called Verdie to tell her I was leaving, she asked me if

I'd seen anyone fitting Marcus's description hanging around. She was worried because he was a stranger. She did mention that Parker's partner, George, had questioned her about everyone at the restaurant that morning. She had to tell him, so he'd be on the lookout for someone fitting Marcus's description."

"And I showed up at the police station," Marcus replied, hitting himself on the forehead. "We should have sent Roark instead."

"*I* should have sent Roark instead," Jackson shot back, getting up to pace around the room. "If Verdie mentioned you to Andrews, well...then he'd naturally let Parker know you were there. Parker followed you to check you out."

"But *he* killed Meredith," Eloise said. "Why would he want to question Marcus?"

"Maybe he's hoping to find someone to pin this on," Marcus offered. "And I looked like a good choice—stranger lurking about, flirting with the help, asking questions. It's just enough to take the heat off himself for a while." He shrugged. "I didn't break protocol, Jackson, I promise. But the café wasn't very busy that morning and I did kind of stand out as being new in town." Then he winked. "I mean, what can I say? People notice me."

Jackson's glowering look stopped Marcus's boasting. "Obviously, Verdie noticed you and so did the Martino bunch. Haven't I taught you anything?"

"Hey, I did my job," Marcus said, all teasing aside. "I was dressed completely different today. I know how to stay undercover, sir."

Jackson pushed a hand through his hair. "You're right. I'm sorry. It was my call and I blew it. I should have sent Roark to talk to the police. I take full responsibility."

Eloise stood up. "Look, this could have all been an innocent mistake. Verdie wants to find out who killed Meredith as much as I do and she probably gave the police any information she could remember. She was just trying to cooperate."

"And we have to go on the assumption that she told Andrews about everyone who'd been by the diner that week," Jackson added, hoping to smooth Marcus's obvious anger. Then he had another thought. "Maybe someone else was watching the café that morning, too. And maybe that someone saw you there, recognized you and spilled the beans. Or just reported back to Martino."

He looked at Marcus. Marcus lifted his head. And they both said in unison, "The leak." They'd been so careful, but if the wrong person had seen their internal memos and identified them...

"I'll call Micah right now," Jackson said, thinking if someone from the Marshal's office had gained access to his task force in Billings, that same someone would have told Martino where to find the entire team. And... Eloise.

She turned, her gaze locking with his. Jackson gave her a reassuring look then headed upstairs to call his brother.

Micah answered on the second ring. "Jackson? Everything okay?"

"No," Jackson said, explaining about Marcus being

made. "He had both Parker and some Martino men on his tail but he lost them."

Micah let out a sigh. "So you think someone told Martino exactly where Eloise lives?"

"It's beginning to look that way. No one in Snow Sky knows any of us, but two suspicious men sure spotted Marcus at the police station today and from the descriptions it sounds like the same two who attacked Verdie at the café. I have a feeling they've been by Eloise's town house, too. Which means our leak is still passing on information. If it's Sellers, we need to watch him even closer."

"I'm doing that," Micah said. "He's not making any moves right now—but then, if he's told them your location he wouldn't need to."

"Has he been away from the office recently?"

"I'd have to check on that. I'll find out."

"What about the decoy?"

"We're working on that angle," Micah said. "We can't just rush in, though. If he knows everything about our operation, he'd get suspicious. Especially if he already knows what you're doing. We've dropped some hints but we have to set up the paper trail so he'll have a reason to have access to the information through official channels, not just because we shove it at him."

"Good point," Jackson said. "Just keep at it and try to lure him out."

"I'll keep you posted," Micah said. "Hey, Jackson?"

"Yeah?"

"I got a call from Zane Black. He and Kristin are

fine but…she's asking about her mother. I told him I'd pass it on. Maybe you could give them a call, update them that Eloise is safe."

"I'll do that," Jackson said, remembering a conversation he'd had with Zane a few weeks ago. "Zane gave a strong indication that the leak might be coming from your office. Maybe I can jog his memory, too, while I'm at it."

"Let me know if you find anything that can help us pin down Sellers."

Jackson hung up then dialed Zane's number.

"We're good," Zane said. "But she's worried. She won't plan the wedding until she knows her mother will be able to come. I could use some help here, Jackson."

"It's too risky right now," Jackson said, "but maybe I can arrange a quick phone call. I'll let you know, okay?"

"Okay. How are things on your end?"

"Not so good. We think the leak might have sent Martino's men right to Eloise's door. Did you ever figure out what you had on your mind when we last talked about the possibility of a leak?"

Zane inhaled a breath. "I don't know. I guess I was just so worried about Kristin I was grasping at straws, but…I keep thinking about the two marshals who came to the Westbrook police station right after someone tried to push Kristin into traffic. One of them—he just kept staring at Kristin. At the time, I thought probably because she resembled some of the women they were investigating. Like I said, it nagged me, but since then I kinda let it go. I mean, they'd be interested in the case, of course, but this guy looked almost angry."

A red flag went up in Jackson's mind. "Can you describe him?"

Zane was silent for a minute. "I think so. He looked to be in his late forties. Graying brush-cut hair, hazel eyes." He let out a grunt. "And…he walked with a limp."

"A limp? You're sure."

"Yeah, he walked right by us," Zane said. "And he never took his eyes off Kristin."

"Thanks," Jackson said, whirling to stare down at Eloise. "I'll get back to you about that phone call."

He called Micah back. "Hey, doesn't Sellers have a disability?"

"Yes, he was injured a few years ago—used to be a field agent. Why?"

"Zane Black just identified someone matching his description as being in the Westbrook police station the same day Zane and Kristin were there. Said he showed a strong interest in Kristin."

"I think we have our man." Micah replied, his tone curt. "Seems Sellers took a half day off a few days back."

Jackson inhaled sharply. "Let me guess? The same morning Marcus was stationed at Ellie's Café, right?"

"Yep. Claimed he had a doctor's appointment across town. Haven't verified that yet, but I'm thinking he did a quick trip up to Snow Sky, probably to meet with the Mob."

"Staked out the diner then recognized Marcus sitting inside."

"Looks that way." Micah lowered his voice. "He probably left quick when the police showed up. I'll set up the sting ASAP. Maybe we should plant the decoy in Eloise's apartment then I'll make sure Sellers has access to that information through the proper channels. Then we wait."

"Do that," Jackson said. "And keep me posted."

He put away his phone then looked back down at Thea and Eloise. If they could take down Sellers, that would be one problem solved at least.

But he had two other problems.

Parker was still after Eloise.

And so was Martino.

No matter what, he couldn't let either one of them get to her. Because they were both desperate and dangerous and neither of them had much to lose at this point.

While Jackson had everything to lose.

NINE

"What do we have?"

Eloise watched as the team gathered around Jackson at the breakfast table. It was early morning and the sun was spilling over the distant mountains with a brightness that belied the dark mood inside the mountain retreat.

"Autopsy shows Meredith Parker died from a massive skull fracture," Roark said, handing over the report he'd downloaded earlier. "If he pushed her, then she landed almost headfirst when she fell from the top of the landing." He glanced at Eloise. "I won't go into all the technical details, but the report indicates the body was moved after death."

Eloise couldn't stop the gasp of horror. She covered her mouth with one hand then looked away.

Jackson looked up at Eloise. "That doesn't give us much to work with, though. She could have fallen by accident."

"She wasn't moved by accident," Eloise shot back.

Roark leaned forward. "There's more, sir. The pathologist report shows signs of old trauma on the body—broken bones in one wrist, some scars and just-healing contusions on the face and a hairline fracture to the right jawline."

"Any trace evidence or DNA comparisons?" Jackson asked.

"Just some hairs and yes, some of them match Parker. But then, we know he's the spouse and that complicates pinning down trace matter as evidence. Besides, he's already been questioned and ruled out as a suspect since he was technically on a stakeout that night."

"Has anyone questioned his partner?"

Roark nodded. "I talked to the captain this morning. That's the sticking point. Seems the partner left the vehicle and watched the perp from another location for about an hour. They were afraid the perp was going to run."

"So…the partner is probably covering for him. And no one else knows for sure if Parker stayed near the stakeout."

"I know," Eloise said. "He left and came home. I saw him standing over her body. He didn't stay on his job that night."

"But we can't use what you saw yet," Jackson reminded her. "And even if he was standing over her body, that won't wash in court. We need to pin down George Andrews."

"With or without Andrews to back him up, Randall Parker beat her," Eloise said from her spot in the kitchen. "And he threw her off that landing."

When everyone turned around to stare at her, she dropped her hand down to the counter. "I'm sorry. I know you're all used to talking in technical terms, but

I worked with Meredith every day and…I saw how she tried to cover up the bruises. I remember when she came in to interview for the job, she was wearing a cast on her wrist. She told me she fell on a hiking trip. I had no reason to doubt her, but later…I figured it all out." She slumped toward the counter. "I should have done more—"

"You tried," Jackson said, getting up to refill his coffee cup, his eyes returning to her again and again. "And you're here now, helping us to piece things together."

"He can't get away with this," she said, her mind whirling as she relived the nightmares she'd had last night.

Jackson stood there, staring at her, then turned toward Roark and Thea. Marcus was outside standing watch around the property.

"What else? Anything on the rope or the roses? And have we managed to narrow down the two capos hanging around?"

Thea nodded. "Roses are hard to come by in Montana, but we found a couple of local florists who have them shipped in from farms around the country. One had an order for red roses two days ago and the other one didn't remember any rose orders in the last few days. Neither had any white roses with pink-edged tips on-site. Said they are rare and hard to find since they aren't standard."

"So Martino could have had them shipped in," Jackson said. "Which means our leak gave Martino's men Eloise's exact location."

Thea nodded then continued. "And on those capos—from Verdie's description one of them could possibly be Ernest Valenti—he's Vincent's right-hand man."

Jackson grunted. "Vincent would be nearby, then. Valenti's been loyal to the family since he first came on board when Vincent was just a baby."

He'd inched closer to her somehow, Eloise realized. She could feel the warmth of his eyes on her. He didn't want to put her through this, but it was his job, after all.

Deciding she should truly help them instead of standing here reliving nightmares, Eloise glanced up at him. "Salvatore did grow the most beautiful roses. He had a greenhouse at the back of the Martino compound. I remember Danny talking about that place and how Salvatore would brag on his prize-winning roses. I'm sure someone is still in charge of their upkeep. Vincent could have roses shipped directly from his own garden or the greenhouse. Knowing him, he probably has a rose farm somewhere."

Roark hit the table with his palm. "We could send some of the petals to our lab, sir. Have them analyzed there. They could probably get a close match if they compared them to any registered hybrids." He shrugged when Jackson shot him an amused glance. "Hey, my mom grows roses so I know a little about how it works."

Eloise nodded. "He's right. Salvatore would have registered his hybrid to establish the trademark. He entered them in flower shows all over Illinois. If he ever won, there might be a record somewhere. But then, he might have sent a representative to enter the shows for him."

"Good suggestion," Jackson said, his tone low. But his eyes shined brightly as he studied her face. "Let's take a break."

And just like that, Eloise found herself being escorted to the enclosed sunroom at the back of the house.

"This is hard," Jackson said, closing the French door behind them so they were alone.

Eloise stared out over the trees and the sloping foothills. The jagged rock faces contrasted sharply with the ponderosa pines and yellow and fuchsia wildflowers lining the slopes and meadows. The stream that flowed behind the cabin gurgled with tiny whitecaps as it washed over the rock bed. She could hear it through the open screen windows. And farther around the curve in this particular outcropping of rocks and trees, the nearby falls swirled and plunged toward the Missouri River.

"Yes, it's hard." She looked over at him. "But you don't need to protect me, Jackson. I'm used to this, remember?"

The sympathy in his eyes almost made her come unglued. "You shouldn't be used to it. No one should have to live like this."

"But you do, don't you? You eat, drink and breathe this stuff, every day."

"Yeah, well, there's always retirement."

"You'd never retire," she said, wondering what he'd do with his life if he gave up the FBI.

"I've never considered it…until now," he said, his shimmering eyes holding her. "I've never had a reason to give up my job but…this case…all these months of trying to stay one step ahead of Martino, it's getting to me. And I'm getting older by the minute."

It was her turn to feel sympathetic. "You don't look that old to me."

He pointed to his temple. "Have you noticed this touch of gray in my hair?"

She looked him over, taking her time, savoring this quiet intimacy. "I've noticed a lot about you."

He lifted one eyebrow—a habit she'd noticed about him. "And?"

"And—I have no complaints. I never did."

He smiled at that. "You look as pretty as ever, even with those contacts you wear now. I miss your green eyes."

"I've had to keep up the disguise so long I don't even think about it anymore. I don't wear a lot of makeup and I can't remember the last time I put on a pretty dress. I have to downplay everything."

"You don't want to bring attention to yourself—it's a survival instinct."

"Yes. I wore a scarf most days in the restaurant, to keep my hair off my face and to also keep my hair covered as much as possible. I always look downright frumpy, on purpose."

"And I've always found you downright beautiful—on purpose."

She looked away, the heat of his gaze searing her

in the same way the sun was bouncing off the rocks below.

"When I kissed you the other night," he started then stopped. "When we kissed, did that make you feel uncomfortable?"

That was a loaded question. She stared down at the stream so long she saw white spots when she looked back up. "I'm not sure. I mean, it was a surprise. A pleasant surprise." She avoided looking at him.

"I shouldn't have done that."

Her head came up. "Why did you?"

"I just wanted to," he said in his straightforward Jackson way. "I just needed to. It's been so long."

"Did you think you'd get it all out of your system?"

"I'll never get you out of my system," he said, turning so abruptly she felt the air swishing past her.

"We'd better get back inside."

Eloise stood there for a minute, shocked but not so surprised. This was pure Jackson. Blunt, brisk and honest. Nothing barred, but nothing exposed, either. She wanted to call him back, to kiss him again. To show him that if she had her way they'd ride off into their own sunset together and all the horror and ugliness they'd both seen would be behind them.

But she didn't have her way. So she resorted to the one prayer she'd held in her heart since he'd shown up on her doorstep. *Lord, keep him and my daughter safe. No matter what, Lord. Keep them both in Your loving arms, protected and safe.*

* * *

Jackson did a head roll and touched a hand to his aching neck. He was exhausted but he had to keep moving, to keep thinking this thing through. At least things had been quiet today. No sign of anyone lurking about and no phone calls with dire news. But even the quiet made him antsy.

Marcus let out a yawn from his chair across from Jackson. "Everything's set for the sting, sir. Decoy should be in place by morning and Micah and his team have set things in motion with the proper paperwork and a dummy meeting in the Marshal's office. It's all been cleared with the Chief Marshal. It might take a few days for our man to make his move, but I'm thinking we should have this all tidied up by week's end."

"Thanks, GQ," Jackson said. "Just keep me posted."

"Micah is doing a great job," Marcus replied. "He's a lot like you, you know."

"He's a lot like our father," Jackson countered. "Stubborn and determined."

"And like I said, he's a lot like you."

Jackson accepted the grin that came with that comment and smiled back at Marcus. "You think I'm stubborn?"

"It's one of your most endearing qualities, sir."

"And do you think I'm determined?"

"On this case, more than ever, sir."

They sat silent for a few minutes, the ticking of the grandfather clock in the foyer the only sound. Roark was on night duty and Thea was guarding Eloise as usual, Duff with them in the bedroom upstairs.

Marcus cleared his throat and stretched his legs out toward the pine coffee table. "You care about her, don't you?"

Not sure how to answer that, Jackson stared at the empty fireplace. "I care about all the people I'm sworn to protect."

Marcus let that slide but he didn't give up. "But you have a history with Ms. Smith. I'm just wondering does that make this job worse for you."

"What do you think?" Jackson asked, unable to give out any more information—out of respect for Eloise.

"Okay, I get it. You don't want to talk about this."

"No, I don't," Jackson replied. "But…if you're worried about me slipping up again like I did the other day when I sent you to the police station, you can relax. That's not going to happen again."

"You know your job, sir," Marcus replied. "I'd never even suggest otherwise."

"But?"

"But, it's none of my business. I just…worry."

"You, worry?" Jackson laughed. "You're as cool as they come, GQ."

"Yeah, I am that." Marcus grinned again. "But I like having you as my boss and I'd hate for that to go bad."

"Ah, do you need a hug?" Jackson asked, going sappy as he grinned back.

"No, sir." Marcus got up then whirled to stare down

at him. "But I don't need to go to your funeral, either. I'm watching your back—we all are."

Jackson couldn't find a comeback for that one. "Thanks. I appreciate that. But…I'm still in charge and I won't let any of you down."

"I never doubted that, sir."

"Well, I have at times," Jackson admitted. "Now, get some sleep."

Marcus saluted then headed up the stairs.

While Jackson sat warring between going back over everything involved in this case or just sitting and thinking about the woman he'd been involved with because of this case.

The two went hand in hand, unfortunately. And the two had colored and shaped his whole career. Was he coming full circle here? He stood up to stare out at the night, the yellow security light showing him the angles and ridges of the mountains and trees. Roark was out there somewhere, walking and watching.

Back in Chicago, Jackson had a bird's-eye view from his fourth-floor office window of a church steeple sitting amongst the buildings and skyscrapers. He could always just see the top of the shimmering white steeple, the part where the white filigree iron cross stood out in stark contrast to the drab buildings around it.

How many times had he stood there, staring at that cross, watching and praying?

Watch and pray. But he wasn't much of a praying man.

Jackson remembered his dad telling him that once

when he asked about being a cop. "How do you do it, Dad? How do you do such a dangerous job?"

"Watch and pray, son," his dad had responded. "Watch and pray."

Now it seemed Jackson had been watching for years, but he'd never prayed that much. Until now. Now his haphazard, rusty prayers echoed through his mind in a steady cadence. "Help me to do my job. Help me to keep her safe. Take care of Kristin and Zane. Let them find a happy life together. Protect my team...and me. Only so we can keep her safe."

He had to concentrate on that—keeping Eloise safe. So he would watch and pray. Day and night, until he knew for sure he'd done his job. Before he could focus on the woman, he had to keep focused on the case. But once he had Martino locked up and he'd brought Randall Parker to justice, well, then he intended to give his full attention to Eloise. Only Eloise, one way or another.

Eloise struggled to breathe.

The dream was back. The suffocating dream where she was running in the night and she was alone and filled with terror. She could hear Duff barking somewhere in the background, could hear heavy footsteps behind her. Then she was lost in a maze of rosebushes. They shot to the sky, their branches lush with blossoming white petals and heavy spiked thorns. The pink tips of the roses turned to blood, dripping like teardrops as she hurried by. She could smell the roses, feel the cut from the thorns.

Then she heard a scream and Meredith calling out to her. "Help me, Eloise. Help me, please."

"I'm coming."

The words Eloise tried to scream were held silent inside her head. And the footsteps were getting closer and closer behind her.

Then a face appeared in front of her. Vincent Martino—the younger version she remembered so long ago and the older version of the man today. He laughed as he reached for her. Then he changed into Randall Parker, jeering at her. "I need to talk to you!"

But Meredith was no longer screaming. The screams turned to a baby crying and then a young woman calling out to her. "Mommy. Mommy, please don't leave me."

Kristin. Kristin was calling for her.

Eloise woke up and her own screams filled the night.

Jackson shot out of bed, grabbed his gun and ran toward the door to the bedroom, the bone-chilling sound of a woman's cries and Duff's excited barks piercing his soul. "Thea?"

Thea opened the door, alert but bleary-eyed, her own weapon held close. "It's all right, sir. Just a bad dream."

Eloise rushed past Thea and right into Jackson's arms.

"I...I... He was after me."

Jackson held her close then motioned for Thea to

leave them alone. Glancing behind him, he did the same with Marcus. "Tell Roark everything's okay."

Marcus nodded then turned back to his room, shutting the door behind him.

"Come sit down," Jackson said, guiding her to the big chair by the daybed.

Eloise sank down then looked up at him, her green eyes wide with fear, her hands shaking as she brushed at her hair. "I'm such a baby but it was horrible. So real."

"You had a bad dream," he said. "That doesn't make you a baby. It obviously shook you to wake you like that."

"I woke the whole house."

"It's okay. That's what we're here for."

She glanced around, blinking. "It was just a dream."

"Yes." He looked her over. "Take a deep breath and tell me about it."

"Everything was all mixed up in my mind," she said. "Martino, Parker, Meredith. The roses, everywhere. And blood." She grabbed his hand. "The roses were crying blood, Jackson. And I felt as if all of that blood was on my hands. All those women who died because they looked like me. Meredith. And then—" She stopped, tears flowing down her face. "And then, I heard a baby crying. My baby. Kristin. But then the baby changed to a child, begging me not to leave." She grabbed at his cotton T-shirt, her eyes wet and wild. "Jackson, how could I do that? How could I leave my baby?"

Jackson didn't answer. Instead, he scooped her up into his arms and turned, settling into the chair as he held her there and let her cry. She'd been holding this in for so long, he wondered how she'd stayed sane. But then he remembered she had the faith to move mountains.

And she'd moved a lot of mountains in her lifetime.

"I've got you," he said, his lips touching her hair and her face. "I've got you now, Ellie. And I won't let go, I promise."

"I...I want to see her, Jackson. Please let me see my daughter."

Her plea tore through all of his resolve, breaking him in half with its intensity. He couldn't honor her request right now. It was too dangerous.

"I'll see what I can do," he said, meaning it. He'd figure something out.

She held to him, her sobs turning to silent tears. "Thank you."

He looked down at her, saw her as the young girl he'd fallen for then saw her as the woman he would always love.

Then he kissed her cheek, the feather of his lips against her warm skin bonding them together with a silent promise.

"I've got you," he said again. "Go back to sleep."

As he held her there, Jackson could almost feel God's presence around them, telling them both the same thing.

He closed his eyes and prayed God was holding them in His arms. He sure could use that kind of strength right now.

TEN

"Roark, are you in place?"

"Affirmative. I'm in the park in front of the apartment, sir."

"Okay, stay cool," Jackson said, his pulse beating like a landslide against his temple. "We've got to make this work."

"Yes, sir."

He turned inside the SUV. "I'm glad you're here."

His brother, Micah, nodded, the tense look on his face mirroring the tension tightening inside Jackson's stomach. The decoy agent was in place along with two others who were hiding inside the apartment. If the Martino men showed up, they could be pretty sure Sellers had tipped off the Mob, and that he'd been the leak the whole time. He was the only outside agent who'd been clued in on this particular setup—on purpose.

"Let's hope we end this thing," Micah replied, his dark eyes alert in the predawn light. "We just have to see if Sellers fell for the bait."

"And hope Sellers tells us where Martino is since he seems to have disappeared off the radar once again."

"He's like a rat," Micah replied. "They slink away when the light's too bright."

Jackson trained his eyes on Eloise's apartment. The decoy had gone into place late last night. The leak wouldn't know that two junior agents were also in place. That wasn't the point, after all. The point was that if Martino's men showed up then they'd know Sellers was their man.

And they'd question him and the thugs until they told them everything they needed to know.

"So how are things with you and Jade?" he asked Micah to fill the time and take his mind off what might go wrong.

Micah grinned. "Great. We're planning the wedding."

"Everybody's talking weddings. Clay, Kristin..." Jackson shot back, an image of Eloise coming down an aisle toward him floating through his frazzled mind. "I haven't had much of a chance to congratulate you. But I'm happy for you."

"Thanks." Micah looked as if he wanted to say more but he didn't. Seconds ticked by, then he asked, "How come you never married?"

"This," Jackson replied. "Who'd want to marry a man who spends most of his time casing a suspect?"

"Good point. But...I'm giving it a shot. I love her."

Jackson could understand that feeling but maybe he wasn't as brave as Micah in the love department. "Don't do as I've done. If you love her, go for it. I'm behind you if this is what you want." He looked over at his little brother—now a fully grown man. "Did I tell you I'm glad you're here?"

"About three times already," Micah said, grinning. "I just hope this is over with soon so I can get on with my wedding."

Jackson thought about Kristin and Zane. It seemed a lot of people were caught in limbo because of this case. He'd been in limbo since the first time Eloise had walked out of his life. Maybe this time, things would turn out differently. "Me, too."

Micah tapped at the dashboard. "Hey, Jackson, I need to ask you something."

Jackson slanted a look toward him. "You don't sound so sure."

"I'm sure," Micah replied. "I just hope you'll feel sure about it, too."

"Okay, ask, then."

"Will you be my best man?"

Jackson swallowed the lump forming in his throat. "I...uh...I'd be honored."

"Really?"

"Of course." He wanted to add that it all depended on how this case ended, but he was going to think positively on that for his brother's sake. "I'll be there."

Micah grinned then slapped his arm. "Don't worry. We aren't planning anything until this mess is cleared up. And we don't want a big wedding."

"That's what they all say," Jackson replied with his own smile. "I really am happy for you, though."

Micah acknowledged that with a nod. "What's gonna

happen with you and Eloise—I mean, if we do end this thing soon?"

"I don't know," Jackson said, being honest. "We'll have to wait and see. Speaking of that, I'm gonna check in with Thea and Marcus."

Thea answered on the second ring. "Yes, sir?"

"Just checking."

"We're fine. She's still asleep and Marcus is patrolling."

"Good. She didn't get much rest yesterday."

"The house is locked up tight and the alarm is set," Thea replied. "Duff is standing guard with me."

"Be careful," Jackson said. "Don't let her out of your sight. And check in with Marcus every fifteen minutes."

"Yes, sir."

He hung up then glanced over at his brother. "What?"

"I think I know exactly what's gonna happen between you and Eloise when this is over," Micah said. Then he started humming the wedding march.

While Jackson remembered holding Eloise in his arms, watching her fall asleep.

"I shouldn't have left her," he said.

"You mean way back then?"

He didn't want to get into "way back then." "No, this morning. I had no choice, though. I wanted to be in on this sting."

"Thea's capable, isn't she? And Marcus might be all preppy but he can get downright nasty in a fight."

"Very capable, both of them. But...still, I can't help but worry."

"Maybe you'll be back there sooner than you think."

Jackson nodded then heard static crackling in his ear.

Roark's voice came through. "We got action at the apartment, Big Mac. Looks like it's showtime."

"He did show his roses!"

Thea turned from the laptop, her face beaming with pride. Eloise came to stand behind her, the Web shot of the lush white roses clustered in a crystal vase making her feel nauseated. "Secret Crush?"

"That's the name of his rose, ma'am," Thea said, pointing to the caption. "'The Martino family of Chicago takes credit for this showstopper. Created by one of Salvatore Martino's own rose growers, the Secret Crush represents everything a white rose stands for—purity, innocence, charm and secrecy. Sometimes called the silent rose, a white rose is usually used for weddings. The Secret Crush is considered a top hybrid and is often sent to remind people of how much they are missed.'"

She stopped, a hand going to her throat. "Maybe that was the message Martino wanted you to hear, ma'am."

"He wanted to silence me, that's for sure." Eloise leaned against the balcony banister. "He *misses* the fact that his father didn't kill me long ago. The old man's dead now. Why can't Vincent let it go?"

"It's a matter of honor—a sick logic, but Vincent

wants to avenge his father," Thea said, turning back to the computer. "But the roses might be his downfall. If we can prove the roses we found in your yard are Secret Crush roses, then that places him or someone within his organization at your apartment. 'Cause I don't think a delivery person would bring them in the middle of the night and just drop them over the fence like that." She hit a button. "I'll print this out for Jackson to see and in the meantime, I'm going to do a search for rose farms where these might be grown. The Martino family must use the farms as a legitimate business cover, but who knows what else they grow on their farms."

"You don't think—"

Thea turned to look up at her. "When it comes to the Mafia, you can't be too careful or too sure, ma'am. They have ways of hiding things that make it very difficult to pin anything on them."

Eloise stared at the picture on the screen. "I'll never look at roses in quite the same way."

"You'd be wise to remember that," Thea replied. Then she looked embarrassed and started shuffling papers. "I mean, there are lots of other flowers around to make you forget roses."

Eloise felt sorry for the other woman. She wanted to keep her subject calm and quiet but Thea also wanted to bond with Eloise in a feminine way. Being a woman FBI agent couldn't be easy. And neither was being the heavily guarded subject. They were in this together now, though. And apparently neither of them ever slept very much.

Eloise glanced around toward the windows. It was

shaping up to be a beautiful summer day and she longed to take Duff for an early-morning walk, but she'd been warned by Jackson to stay inside until he got back.

"I hope we hear from them soon," she said as she paced toward the upstairs dormer window in the corner of the loft. "Shouldn't we have heard something by now?"

Thea turned in her chair. "I'm used to waiting out things like this, but I guess you're not, huh?"

"No, and it's driving me a little nuts."

"He knows how to stay safe, Ms. Smith."

"Does he?" she asked, whirling. "How has he done it all these years?"

Thea gave her a direct look. "Well, for one thing, he stays in shape and he stays current. He knows the latest technology and he stays in training. Many mornings, I'll get to work early to go for a jog around Lake Michigan but I'll always find him coming back from his jog. Same at the gun range. He's there all the time. He's always one step ahead of everybody else."

"Except Martino."

"Well, he's working on that one, too." Thea stopped, looking unsure. "You know about the Veiled Lady, right?"

"He told me about her, yes. Do you have any idea who she is?"

"No, but I think Jackson does. He won't say, though. He's honoring her request to only speak to him. She calls him sometimes and she meets with him in very secret locations. If it hadn't been for this informant, a lot more women might be dead."

"But…someone is also tipping off the Mob? Could it be her?"

"We've checked on that and investigated it. We can't identify this woman but we can't pin her to any leaks with the Mob, either. She'd be crazy to even attempt double-crossing Jackson or the Mob."

"Somebody is, though," Eloise said, her anxiety increasing by the minute. "What if Jackson and the other agents are the ones being set up this morning?"

Thea got up. "Ma'am, you're just creating worry where there shouldn't be any. All we can do right now is sit tight and wait this out. I'm sorry I can't offer you more hope."

Eloise nodded. "I'm going to the kitchen."

"Yes, ma'am. I've got some more work to do here."

"That's fine. You keep working. I'll make breakfast and maybe bake some cookies."

Thea gave her an indulgent smile. "I'm going to gain five pounds before this is over."

"I hope so," Eloise said in parting. "That way I'll know you're okay and being taken care of."

"Hey, I'm the one who's supposed to be taking care of you," Thea replied.

But Eloise couldn't deal with that. She wasn't used to being taken care of. She'd been on her own so long, she didn't know anything else but loneliness and silence. She'd turned to God in her darkest hours and now, she turned to Him again. Her prayers brought her comfort but her mind whirled with worry about everything that could go wrong.

I can't love him, she thought, her mind on Jackson.

It's too hard to love a man who stays in constant danger. I can't love him.

But she did. And…she might have to add that to her prayer list. She might need to ask God to help her get over loving Jackson. If he could reunite her with her daughter, she could live with that. So she asked God to help make that happen. She couldn't ask for anything more.

"Who is that?"

Jackson squinted in the morning light as a lone figure emerged out of the shadows near Eloise's apartment.

Micah leaned forward. "I don't recognize him."

"Roark?"

"Here, boss."

"Who's our early-morning visitor?"

Roark grunted. "It's Parker, sir. What's he doing here?"

Jackson hit the steering wheel. "I don't know but he's gonna blow everything if we don't get him out of here."

"Do you think someone tipped him off that Ms. Smith is back?" Roark countered.

"Who? How?" Jackson's frustration echoed over the two-way. "I can't believe this."

"He's probably been watching the place," Roark replied. "He might be onto us, too."

"Along with about half this town and the Mafia, obviously." Jackson quickly filled in Micah. "We've got double trouble if the Mob shows up. They won't like a witness hanging around. We could have another murder on our hands."

Giving instructions to the team and the decoy, Jackson waited and watched. Parker was definitely snooping. He kept glancing around, checking the scene. Was the man going to break in to talk to the woman he thought was Eloise?

Roark cut through the line. "If the Martino clan shows up now, they'll bolt. Or kill Parker in the process of trying to get to our decoy."

"Tell me something I don't know," Jackson retorted. "Move in and wait." He warned the decoy and the other agents inside the town house to be on the alert.

"This man has caused me nothing but trouble," he told Micah. "We think he's after Eloise, but we can't do anything about it. We're already pushing the envelope doing our little investigation of him on the side."

Micah watched the complex. "Should we move in and grab him out of the way?"

"Not yet," Jackson said, training his eyes on Parker. "He might go away on his own."

He'd just finished that sentence when the action across the way picked up. Too late, Parker turned from the door just as a car sped up the tiny driveway. Two men got out and rushed toward Parker. He was trapped.

"Just perfect," Jackson hissed. "Stand down!" He drew his gun, watching for a few minutes. But Parker was getting more belligerent by the minute. And so were the two thugs. Parker barked questions while the thugs shouted back nonanswers. "We're moving in but hold your fire."

Carefully, he and Micah opened the SUV doors and slipped out to hide behind a clump of shrubbery. "He'll scare them off if he tells them who he is." And it would be just like the blustery Parker to announce his rank.

Jackson watched as Parker argued with the men. One man pushed at the detective and then things turned ugly. Parker drew a gun and aimed it at the taller of the two, shouting all the while that he wanted details about Ellie Smith. But the other henchman was just as fast and probably just as mean. He drew his own gun and held it on Parker.

"It's over," Jackson hissed, recognizing the man as Ernest Valenti. "We can't get caught in the middle of this, but we need to keep those two soldiers alive for questioning." He quickly filled in the team. "That's one of Vincent Martino's right-hand men—Ernest Valenti."

Roark spoke into the line. "You won't believe this, sir. They're comparing notes on Eloise Smith. And none of them are giving anything up. This can't be good."

Just what he'd feared the most, Jackson thought. Parker and the Mafia putting two and two together. And both of them wanted Eloise dead.

"What do you want us to do?" Marcus asked. "We've got the agents inside the house ready to move."

"Tell them to stay inside." Jackson watched as Parker held his gun high and tried to get past one of the men. And then he heard a gunshot.

After that, everything turned even nastier and Jackson had to think quickly. If Detective Randall Parker was found dead on Eloise's doorstep after mouthing off about her all over the airwaves, she'd become a prime suspect in both his murder and his wife's and every kind of law enforcement would be looking for her. Jackson couldn't let that happen.

"We're going in," he said. "We have to stop them before they kill Parker." Then he turned to Micah. "At least we know who our leak is now."

"Sellers," Micah said as they headed toward the ruckus across the way.

ELEVEN

"Roark, stay out of the line of fire," Jackson commanded as he hurried across the street. "And don't shoot to kill. We need to keep them alive."

"I hear that," Roark reported back. He cautioned the decoy and the agents stationed with her to do the same.

Jackson silently commended Roark for his quick thinking. They couldn't afford a shoot-out. But it looked like it was gearing up to become just that.

The two Martino men were backing away, their guns still trained on where Randall Parker lay groaning near the shrubbery by the front window.

Jackson let them keep walking until he was within earshot. "Halt, FBI," he called, his badge out, running now with Micah right behind him. Both of them had their weapons raised and ready.

One of the thugs turned and fired, hitting a tree near Jackson's head. "Micah?" he called, praying his brother hadn't been hit.

"I'm here," Micah shouted, veering off to try and block the way to the Martino vehicle. "I don't think they're gonna cooperate."

He was right. The Martino men weren't going down without a fight. They both started firing and running, taking cover behind trash cans and trees as they hurried to where their haphazardly parked car was waiting with doors wide open.

Roark came running from up the street, his weapon drawn. "Stop! FBI!"

Those were not the words the Martino men wanted to hear a second time. They kept shooting, forcing Jackson and Micah to duck behind a stone statue at the entrance to the park. Bullets hit the solid rock of the statue, pinging off and ricocheting back into the air.

Jackson hazarded a glance to where Roark had taken cover behind a huge oak tree. "This isn't going very good," he said to Micah, his breath winded.

Micah did a quick reload. "Not like we'd planned, no."

Parker let out another moan and lifted up, firing his own weapon. One of Martino's men ducked, cursing as the bullet pierced his lower leg. Blood started pouring out, but he held his weapon steady as he found cover.

And now, all over the neighborhood, lights were coming on and people were peeking out their doors while dogs locked inside fences barked frantically.

"Stay inside. FBI!" Roark called. As doors slammed shut, he was rewarded with another round of fire from one of Martino's men.

Parker got up, crouched and bleeding, as he tried to get to the car. But another round of fire caused him to drop back down behind the shrubbery.

One of the men made it into the car and cranked it,

pulling away as the other one fired his weapon over and over, hoping to hit one of his marks before he hopped into the passenger side and slammed the door. Roark fired back and hit the windshield but that didn't stop the car. It was peeling rubber, the smell acrid and burning in the morning air.

Jackson stepped out, aimed at one of the tires and instead, knocked out a headlight.

And just as the first rays of sun slipped over the horizon, Martino's men were gone in a cloud of smoke and gunfire.

"I got a partial on the plate," Roark said, still trying to catch his breath.

"Good." Jackson looked around Eloise's apartment. The decoy agent was safe and the two junior agents covering her were busy gathering slugs for the ballistic report. Roark was fielding questions from the stunned locals, holding his own with a hostile police force and trying to block any comments to the media.

Parker had been grilled by Captain Lewis as to why he was once again snooping around Eloise Smith's apartment and was now sitting in the ambulance, getting checked over by the paramedics. He'd be on his way to the hospital soon to have a slug removed from his left shoulder. And although Randall Parker had cursed and fussed at Jackson's rapid-fire questions after the Martino men had gotten away, Lewis had promised Jackson another crack at the detective after his surgery.

Parker had a few questions of his own, however. "You haven't told me everything, McGraw. I have a right to know why the FBI is after Ellie Smith. You'd better level with me!"

"I told you to back off," Jackson reminded the man. "You're interfering with a federal investigation, Parker. And you almost got yourself killed this morning."

"I need to find my wife's killer, man."

Jackson had ignored the man's rants for now. He'd talk to Parker and "level" with him, no doubt about that.

Jackson held his hands on his hips, moving in a circle as he assessed the scene. Local cops mingled and merged with FBI agents, while the media was champing at the bit to find out what had happened on such a perfect summer morning in such a serene neighborhood.

"How in the world did we make a mess of this?" he asked anyone who might be listening.

Roark stepped forward. "Uh, sir, we did everything right by the book. Parker, there, got in the way."

"Yes, Parker did get in the way," Jackson agreed. But ultimately, the responsibility of a botched mission fell on Jackson's shoulders. "But we lost our suspects, didn't we?"

"Yes, sir," Roark replied, pushing a hand through his slick brown hair. "My bad."

"Your bad and mine," Jackson replied. "I should have known anybody working for Martino wouldn't just surrender, all meek and mild. They'd rather get shot than make Vincent Martino mad by giving up the goods."

"But…you couldn't just kill them in their tracks without provocation," Micah pointed out, his gaze trained on Jackson. "Jackson, we did all we could. And now, I have men in place to take Mac Sellers in for questioning, and you IDed one of the men as being a top capo. That's a big break for this case."

"It is," Jackson said, his mind whirling. He'd already alerted Marcus and Thea, but he was itching to get back to the safe house and Eloise. "But we didn't get to question the Martino men about that, did we? I'm sure Ernest Valenti would have a lot to say if we could get to him."

Micah ignored that question and instead focused on what he obviously saw was bothering Jackson. "I can question Sellers. He's my man. Let me have him, Jackson."

Jackson nodded. "Okay. Make him talk, Micah. We need evidence and we need to find out all he knows and all he's given to Martino. If he's somehow found out about the safe house—"

"He wouldn't have access to that information," Micah said. Then he shrugged. "Of course, I can't guarantee that."

"That's why I need you to stay on the man," Jackson retorted. "Nothing about this case has been guaranteed and nothing ever goes as planned. I need answers, Micah."

"I'm on my way," Micah said, turning to leave, his head down. Of course, he was probably feeling just as responsible as Jackson right now.

Jackson called him back. "Hey." Micah turned, clearly expecting a few more harsh remarks. "Thanks," Jackson said, lifting one hand in a wave.

Micah didn't reply but he gave his brother a quick, determined glance. Then he turned and headed out to do his job.

Eloise had burned the cookies.

And now, her hands were shaking so hard she couldn't even scrape the residue off the cookie tray.

A shoot-out at her apartment.

She kept hearing those words in her mind. There had been a shoot-out with the Mafia right at her front door, putting her neighbors in danger, putting all the agents in danger. And Randall Parker had been caught in the middle of it. She felt as if a perfect storm was centered over her head and she was about to be tossed and turned until she'd drowned in her own fear and self-loathing.

I should have kept running, she thought over and over, her hands scraping against the crisp stuck-on cookie dough as she tried to dislodge it with an old scouring pad. But in her mind, she was working frantically to break away at all the ugliness that seemed to cling to her. She prayed while she scraped, but she was beginning to believe she wasn't worthy of asking for God's grace.

"Ms. Smith?"

Eloise turned, the scouring pad in one hand, her knuckles cut and bleeding from its frayed wires, to stare at Marcus. "What?"

"Special Agent McGraw is on the line for you, ma'am."

Her body crumbled against the counter, her hand shaking as she dropped the pad and reached out for the cell phone. "Thank you." Trying to find her next breath, she stared at the slick phone.

"Ma'am, he's waiting," Marcus said, stepping back to give her some privacy.

"Hello," Eloise said, her throat as raw and scratchy as the pad she'd been using.

"Ellie?"

Just hearing his voice brought tears of relief to her eyes. "I'm here."

"Are you all right?"

She wanted to laugh. He'd just been through a firestorm and he was asking her if she was okay?

"I'm fine. How about you?"

The touch of sarcasm wasn't lost on Jackson. "I've had better days."

"When…when will you be back here?"

"Soon, I hope. We're clearing things up. Our cover is pretty much blown now, but at least the locals are cooperating. Grudgingly." He went on to explain that'd he'd filled in the police chief and had a briefing with some of the higher-up officers, bringing them up to speed without divulging the essentials of this complicated case. They were on the lookout for the Martino gang but Eloise knew Jackson couldn't rely on that. Parker was very popular within the department and he was gunning for her.

"What about Parker?" she asked, her free hand gripping a sunflower-embossed dish towel.

"He's at the hospital, in stable condition."

"Why was he there this morning, Jackson?"

"We think he's been watching your place and he thought our decoy was you."

"So he had a standoff with the Mafia?"

"Something like that. I'll be there soon and we'll talk more. I just wanted to make sure you're safe."

"I'm fine," she said, relaxing a bit. "Thea and Marcus are making sure of that."

"Good. See you soon."

She stood staring down at the phone for a long time then turned to hand it back to Marcus. "Thank you."

"It's going to be okay," Marcus said.

While Eloise appreciated the reassurance, she knew no one could promise that. So she finished scouring the cookie sheet and rinsed and dried it, then went to the upstairs bathroom to put some lotion on her rough, raw hands. After coming out of the bathroom, she grabbed her Bible and her knitting bag and headed for what was becoming her favorite spot, the big chair centered by one of the dormer windows on the landing. From this vantage point, she'd be able to see Jackson and Roark driving up the mountain road.

And then she'd know for sure he truly was safe.

"We need to go to the hospital to question Parker," Jackson told Roark an hour later. "Then we can get back to the safe house. We'll take the long way so no one follows us."

Roark nodded and put the SUV in Reverse. "We'dda nailed them if Parker hadn't shown up."

Jackson didn't respond. Parker would have figured out by now that there was much more going on here than just the FBI tailing Ellie Smith. Thinking back over this morning, he held two fingers to his nose. This should have gone down without a hitch. Martino's men would have either gained entry to the apartment or would have tried to break in. Either way, once they'd made it inside, Jackson and his agents would have stepped in and taken over—in a quiet, secure fashion, inside the apartment. The two capos would have been surrounded at close range. And things would have ended quietly. Maybe.

But not like this. Not in a public shoot-out that only brought unwanted attention to all of them.

"I blew it," he said to Roark. "I've lost my ability to second-guess Martino. I let Parker get to me, too. I should have alerted him to stay out of the way."

Roark didn't answer, which meant he couldn't say what was on his mind.

"Talk to me," Jackson said. "Tell me what you're thinking, Roark."

Roark glanced over at him then looked back at the road. "It's easy to lose focus when you're preoccupied, sir. At least, that's what you've always taught us."

"Meaning?"

Roark seemed to be weighing his answer. "Meaning, we realize how involved you are in this case. It's personal. I mean, you have a vested interest in seeing this thing through till the end."

"But…what you're really trying to say is that my vested interest is more on Ellie Smith—Eloise Hill—than the real issues here, such as warning Parker before we tried to corner the Mob."

"You do seem to have a soft spot for her, yes."

Jackson neither denied nor confirmed that statement. It was the truth. "What could I have done differently in all of this?"

Roark took a deep breath. "With all due respect, sir, you should have stayed away from Parker. Your visit got his antennae up."

"You all tried to warn me on that."

"But we also understand why you felt it necessary to scare him off. You were trying to protect someone you care about."

"But I shouldn't have mixed FBI business with a local crime case, right?"

"You didn't do the mixing, sir. It was already stewing when you arrived on the scene."

"So, what's your final analysis?"

"This," Roark said, slanting him a long look as they pulled into the hospital parking lot. "What happened this morning was unpredictable. We could stand down and let the mob teach Parker a lesson, or we could move in and try to save a man who might or might not have killed his wife. Either way, we were in a bad position. And that's not really your fault."

Jackson wasn't buying that. "I messed up," he said again. Then he put a hand on the dash. "And I can't afford to do that again."

Because next time, Eloise might be the one to get shot. Or worse, to finally be killed.

And he could never live with that. It would mean the end of his career. Because if that happened, he'd turn in his badge and leave the FBI for good.

Roark didn't have an answer for his declaration so

they made their way into the hospital in silence. But when they got to the front desk, flashing their badges to the two receptionists, Jackson soon realized that his worst fears might be about to come to life.

"Detective Parker is gone, sir," an official-looking administrator who'd been summoned to talk to them explained after some haggling about privacy laws.

"What do you mean, gone?"

"He left the hospital on his own."

Jackson turned to Roark then looked back at the administrator. "In other words, you're telling me Detective Randall Parker is out there somewhere on the loose?"

The man nodded. "Yes, sir. He went through surgery but…when he woke up in the recovery room, he managed to get up and leave without anyone seeing him. I'm afraid he's disappeared. No one can find him."

Jackson looked at Roark and then they both bolted toward the door. No need for words to communicate what they both were thinking.

Both Detective Randall Parker and the Mafia were now on the alert to find Ellie Smith.

And Jackson was in a race against time to get to her before either of them did.

TWELVE

Jackson rushed into the safe house. "Eloise?"

She was already on her way down the open staircase since she'd been by the window, waiting. She'd spotted the black SUV coming up the winding road toward the house and immediately dropped the book she'd been trying to read. "I'm right here."

She watched as a wave of relief washed over him. Meeting him at the bottom of the stairs, Eloise touched his arm. "What is it?"

He went blank, locking his emotions up with a tight control. "Nothing. I was just worried."

Eloise knew he was keeping things from her and she guessed now was probably not the time to ask questions. But she had to know. "What about Parker?"

Jackson's gaze shifted from her face to his agents. "He left the hospital."

Eloise grabbed the newel post. "Left? What do you mean, left?"

"Without being released," Jackson replied. "He's missing."

"Probably on his way out of the country since he's got the Mafia on his case," Roark said.

"But we don't know that, right?" She looked at Jackson. "We don't know where he is, do we?"

He stood there, his hands on his hips, his head lowered, his eyes firmly on her. "No, we don't know where he is. We think his partner helped him leave. No one can locate him, either." He gave her a look that told her he thought he'd failed. "But I'm putting Roark and Marcus on patrol and I'll be personally guarding you—along with Thea."

Eloise let out a breath. "Okay. And what about Martino's men?"

"One's wounded, but we haven't located them yet. We think they're in a rental car, based on the partial license number Roark took, so we're tracing that angle."

"And we've done a check on all local hospitals," Roark said. "No incoming gunshot wounds in the surrounding area. So that means the wound can't be too bad, or they've gone elsewhere to get help."

Thea came running down the stairs. "Sir, I just got a rundown on the murder of Randall Parker's first wife. Our source in Great Falls found some discrepancies from the crime-scene report."

"Such as?" Jackson asked, his eyes on Eloise.

Thea brought him the printout. "A partial shoe print found at the scene. They never could match it at the time of the original crime-scene report. But then later, they matched the print to Detective Parker's athletic shoe and chalked it up to him being there after they found the body, since he was called to the scene to identify his wife. I verified that with the sign-in sheet used at the crime scene."

"Go on."

Thea shook her head. "But, according to this report, Parker *didn't* arrive on the crime scene until *after* the whole place had been swept clean—after they'd brought his wife out, sir. He claimed he was an hour away, on a mountain climb, so it took him a while to get to the scene." She tapped the file. "So this means that Parker had to have been at the scene *before* the CSI team got there to gather evidence—his shoe print proves that because he wasn't wearing the same shoes the day he came to ID his wife. He couldn't have been if he'd been mountain climbing.

"Only no one there connected on this fact. But my source found file photos and newspaper clippings from a reporter who was at the scene—and Parker was still completely dressed in his climbing gear, shoes and all. But, get this, the newspaper photo clearly shows him *behind* the crime-scene yellow tape. He never made it down to the spot where they found her. He IDed her when the paramedics brought her out on a gurney. The picture clearly shows him looking down on the body, but thankfully didn't show the dead woman."

"But it's clear— Are you sure he never went down to the actual spot where the body was found?"

"Witnesses say no."

"Reliable witnesses?"

"Some of the local cops who worked the scene confirmed it when our agent questioned them and so did the newspaper photographer. The cops said they wouldn't let him go down the canyon—he was too distraught and out of control."

"Amazing," Jackson said, shaking his head. "He made a big deal out of it, probably on purpose so they'd do exactly that—hold him back. And so they could testify to that fact, if need be. And the media would see his grief. Only he messed up somewhere."

Thea grunted in agreement. "My source put it together after pouring over the official reports, based on the recorded times on the crime-scene photos and when the reports were filed. Parker wore a special type of athletic shoe sometimes but the day he came to the scene, he's shown wearing an expensive rock-climbing shoe. It wouldn't have left the same sole print even if he *had* gone down the canyon to see his wife's body."

Jackson glanced around. "And no one connected on that fact?"

"Apparently not," Thea said. "Think about it. Detective Parker was supposedly distraught about his wife missing. He rushes to the scene to find her dead, puts on a good show with the grief and shock thing, so why wouldn't they find a partial of his shoe prints all around the immediate scene. Makes sense, unless they identified the wrong shoe…and kind of let it slip that he never was down in the canyon on that day. But he was probably there the day he killed her and dumped her there."

"I'm with you," Jackson said. "So the partial was matched to him and only him?"

"Apparently so," Thea said. "It's all in the report. It was a clean partial since it didn't rain between the time she was killed and dumped there and the time they found her about three days later. If we get this to

Captain Lewis and he can verify it, then we have a solid reason for reopening this case."

Jackson nodded. "Especially if this print happens to match the shoe prints they found where Meredith Parker's body was dumped. I'm guessing it will. But that's a long shot."

"I'll get right on that one, sir," Marcus said.

Eloise had followed the thread but she was still confused. "But that won't help in proving he murdered Meredith."

"It might," Jackson replied. "If he still has those shoes it'll be enough evidence to put him at his first wife's murder scene—*before* they discovered the body. And that will definitely make him a major suspect in his second wife's murder. But only if he still has those shoes or if he even still wears them."

Thea tapped the file. "Maybe he still wears that brand, at least. It means the locals would have a case against him—enough to investigate him in more detail for sure." Then she pointed to a note she'd jotted down. "I found this interesting, too. Remember Parker was on a stakeout the night Meredith died?"

"Go on," Jackson said.

"Remember his partner told Captain Lewis that Parker and he separated that night? After we reported our concerns regarding George Andrews, per our request, Captain Lewis questioned him again. He admitted to the captain that Parker did that a lot on stakeouts—went off on his own and never explained his reasons. The partner's been kind of freaked out about having to cover for him that night—since his wife turned up dead the next day. He divulged all of this off the record, so to speak."

"That is interesting since we're pretty sure Andrews helped Parker leave the hospital," Jackson said. "We need to find both of them. If the partner is willing to talk, we'll have a good case."

Thea nodded. "That's all I have right now, but at least it's a start."

Jackson raked his gaze over the file again. "Good work, Thea. Remind me later to thank our agent in Great Falls. Make sure Captain Lewis gets a copy of this—top secret and top priority—for his eyes only. We have leverage now. We just need our suspect back."

"That is, if the Mafia doesn't find Parker first," Roark reminded them. "And as we all know, they have their own brand of justice."

"But he can't help them," Eloise said. "He just happened to be in the wrong place at the wrong time."

"If they find him and question him," Jackson said, "they could kill him. He was a witness, Ellie, and he's a cop. He saw their faces and he can put them at your apartment this morning."

Eloise let that settle, her mind whirling until a sick feeling pitted like bile in her stomach. "Or...Parker could tell them everything they want to know about me, right? Just to save his own hide."

Jackson's expression went from controlled to grim. "Exactly. And once they get what they want from him, then they'll kill him and come after you. Either way, it's not good. Not good at all."

"But…as far as we know, Parker doesn't have a clue where we're hiding you," Marcus said.

"But we still have to go on the assumption that he might try to track us down," Jackson replied.

"So what do we do now?" she asked, searching his face for signs of reassurance.

"We keep you alive," he said, pulling no punches. "As for the rest, we take it one step at a time until we have both Martino and Parker put away or—" He stopped, turning away to stare over at Roark and Marcus.

She didn't have to read his mind to understand what he hadn't said. *Put away or…dead.*

Two hours later, Jackson's cell rang. The sound brought all the agents and Eloise to the center of the spacious den. Everyone was edgy. Thea had explained about the Martino "Secret Crush" roses, too, so they were waiting to hear about any evidence on that or any word on Parker's whereabouts. Right now, Jackson would be happy to get any news.

He held up a hand for calm and quiet then answered. "Micah? What's up?"

Hearing a collective sigh flowing from all the people around him, Jackson listened to his brother's report.

"Sellers isn't talking. He's more afraid of the Mob than spilling his guts to us. The man's running scared, Jackson. But he's our man—no doubt about that. It's what he's *not saying* that tells the tale."

But they needed a confession. "You can't get anything out of him?"

"Nothing except he needed the cash and he did it

because he felt let down and left out—since his accident and being relegated to desk duty."

"Well, he'll get no sympathy from me."

"Me, either," Micah retorted. "I'm thinking someone made him an offer he couldn't refuse, but until he talks I can't do much else. I'll keep you posted."

Jackson closed his phone then let out a primal yell. Frustration moved with razor-edged sharpness through his veins. His shout-out caused the other agents to move back a step or two. Duff started barking but Thea calmed the dog.

While Eloise stared Jackson down.

"Come with me, please," she said, taking him by the sleeve of his shirt. "Now."

Jackson tried to resist but she held firm. Not wanting to reprimand her in the same way he'd handle one of his agents, Jackson complied. With a frown. His stunned agents stood back, giving each other quizzical, shocked looks, but they didn't interfere.

She took him out onto the sunporch, closing the door behind them. Jackson was well aware that Thea, Marcus and Roark were all watching. But Eloise opened the door and shouted to them, "Don't you people have things to do?"

They scattered like tiny mice.

"Impressive," Jackson said, admiration coloring the word. "What's this about, Eloise?"

"What's this about?" She almost laughed in his face. "I'll tell you what this is about, Jackson. It's about me-specifically you and me. You know, I've prayed for you every day since…since we last saw each other. I prayed for you and for my child. And…sometimes I'd even imagine finding both of you again. Just a silly dream. But never like this—never with the Mob and a bad cop trying to get to me." She stopped, huffed a breath as she stared out over the foothills and mountains. "I can't take much more. But I can't run this time. I know that now. I can't run, Jackson."

"Don't go getting all brave on me, Ellie. You can't go off on your own and face these people—neither Parker nor the mob. I won't let you."

Wanting to convince her, he tried to reach out to her, touch her, but she drew back.

"Don't. Just listen to me. I can't have your death on my conscience, do you understand?"

His gaze locked with hers. "I won't die."

"You don't know that. You can't promise that. They killed Danny. They've killed other women trying to get to me. They could kill you and Kristin. When will it stop?"

"I'm here to protect you," he said, hoping to make her see that he was all right. That *they all* would be all right. "I'm here to make it stop."

She crossed her arms, rubbing her hands against her sweater. "I understand that you think you have a duty to protect me, and I get it every time you leave this house. But…I want you to know now…before anything happens—it's okay, Jackson. I'll be okay if the worst does happen. I have faith that God is in control, not you and certainly not me. God, Jackson. Even if the worst happens. Do you understand me?"

Jackson stepped away, the pain of imagining her

dead too much to bear. He ran a hand through his hair then leaned over to look out at the trees, his knuckles whitening as he pressed his hands against the window-sill. "I will never understand a senseless death, Eloise. Especially not your death. I can't let that happen."

"But you're letting this case get the best of you," she said. "Because of me."

"I know I've made a mess of things," he countered, the shame of that burning through him.

"No," she said, coming to stand beside him. "No, Jackson, you're doing a job, the best job you can do under the circumstances." She put a hand over his, her fingers warm on his tightly curled fingers. "You haven't failed. You didn't mess up. No one could have predicted that Randall Parker would become a part of this equa-tion. And…he's my fault. Mine alone. I should have gone to the police right away. I should have—"

Jackson lifted off the windowsill. "What, Ellie, killed him yourself? Yeah, that would have taken care of things, all right."

"At least I'd have justice," she replied, her tone going from firm and sure to a whisper of despair. "Meredith might be alive if I'd just…done something."

Jackson fell for her all over again. Eloise had always held a high sense of right and wrong. That's why she'd gone against the Mob in the first place. Touching a hand to her face, he said, "Here you are giving me a lecture about not harboring self-imposed notions of guilt and failure, yet you feel the same. And you're trying to take it all on your shoulders." He shook his head. "I'm supposed to be the one protecting you, but you know something, Ellie, you're trying very hard to protect me."

He saw the tears misting her eyes. "Yes, I want to do that. I need to do that. I have to protect you in the only way I know how."

"And how's that?" he asked, drawing her closer with a tug of his hand through her hair.

She didn't pull away this time. Her eyes turned green and misty, like the forest at dawn. "By watching over you. By asking God to watch over you. I've never been one for bargaining with the man above but...if He'll spare you and Kristin, I can live with that."

Jackson hissed a sharp intake of breath, his hand tightening on the back of her neck. "No, you mean you can *die* with that—you're willing to die with that plan? How can God even think about granting that prayer, Ellie?"

"It's the only prayer I have right now," she said, her eyes holding his. "Jackson, are you listening to me?"

Jackson was listening but he didn't plan on going through with that scenario. "You want me to do whatever it takes to protect your daughter, yes, I'm listening. But...I'm telling you, I'm going to live to not only protect Kristin but I'm going to be her mother's date for her wedding." He pulled her into his arms. "That's my prayer, Ellie. That's my one hope and prayer. And...God and I haven't exactly had a clear line of communication but...I'm hoping He'll hear me loud and clear."

With that, he kissed her to show her that he meant business and that he wasn't going to go down without a fight. Not with the Mob, not with Randall Parker.

And certainly not with her.

He was still kissing her when his cell rang again. Pulling away, regret pouring through him, he whispered, "We're not finished here, you hear me?"

She nodded and turned away.

"Hello?"

It was the Veiled Lady.

"You're not safe," came the throaty whisper. "Vincent is getting close. And he's very angry about what happened this morning. He's going to kill you and her, Agent McGraw." He heard a deep sigh and then she said, "Unless I can get there in time to stop him."

THIRTEEN

"Where are you?" Jackson asked, his frustration returning and going into overdrive. While he appreciated this informant, he wished he could get the woman to tell him her true identity. But that had been part of the bargain. No questions about who she really was.

"You know I can't tell you that."

"Look, lady, I need real help here. I've got other problems right now."

"I can only tell you that Vincent is still in Montana and he's searching for Eloise Hill—nothing new there—except he's so mad he's out of control. Someone told him exactly where to find the woman, but as you well know, that discovery didn't pan out. His men are closing in, but he wants to take you out himself, Agent McGraw. He's furious about one of his men getting shot. And he thinks the cop who showed up this morning is part of your sting. So he's not going to send out henchmen anymore. Now he's out on the prowl himself and he wants to be the one to make the kill."

"I get that," Jackson replied, not daring to tell her that Parker was a big part of all of their problems. "If you have any pull with this man, you'll urge him to stop this."

"I have no control. He doesn't even know I exist. Just be forewarned. He's going to find you sooner or later."

The connection ended. Jackson gave Eloise a long stare, the warmth of their earlier kiss giving him courage and reminding him of why he was here. "Let's get inside."

She glanced around. "Are we in danger out here?"

"We're always in danger."

Eloise followed him back into the den. He wouldn't listen to her and he certainly wouldn't tell her what he'd heard on the phone. He'd put himself on the line until the very end. Until it was too late. And she was helpless.

She watched as he shouted out orders. "The Veiled Lady sent us another warning. Martino is getting antsy and he's definitely in the area. Apparently, our little brawl this morning has put him over the edge. He's not issuing orders to his thugs anymore. According to our lady, Martino wants to finish this himself. He's looking for us."

"How does she know all of this if she's never in contact with him?" Roark asked.

"She has to have someone inside the Mob," Jackson replied. "Someone close to Martino. And I think that someone was at Eloise's apartment during the shoot-out."

Marcus whistled low. "Well, I pity that person if Martino gets suspicious."

Jackson nodded. "That's why the Veiled Lady is so afraid to let us know her identity. And that's why Martino doesn't even know she's alive, according to her."

Thea stepped forward. "Sir, could this woman possibly be Vincent's mother? Supposedly, she's dead. But what if—"

Jackson lifted an eyebrow. "Francesca? No. She was killed when she tried to get away from her husband years ago when Vincent was around seven. She had Vincent with her, but they found her, killed her and brought Vincent home. She's dead."

Eloise cleared her throat. "You said this woman told you Vincent doesn't even know she's alive."

Jackson stood stock-still, his mind spinning back over the details of his meetings with the mysterious woman. "Her exact words were that he doesn't even know she exists. I've never seen her face. But she has a raspy voice. Could be an older woman."

"You taped some of the conversations, didn't you, sir?" Thea asked.

"Yes, but that won't help. We don't have Francesca's voice on record anywhere to compare."

"Or he would have done that already," Roark said with an edge.

"I made a deal with the Veiled Lady—that I wouldn't force her to identify herself as long as she dished out information."

"And so she has," Roark said. "But…it's kind of vague. Too bad she can't give us a location on Martino."

"Yeah, too bad," Jackson replied, his tone just as

sarcastic as Roark's. "Maybe she knows but she's afraid to go that far."

"That makes sense. They'd figure it out if she gave details."

"They'd figure out one of their associates or capos has turned traitor," Jackson replied. "And we all know where that leads."

"Bang, bang," Marcus said, his blue eyes icy cold.

Eloise shivered. "If this woman is Vincent's mother, she might be able to get through to him."

Jackson played that scenario in his head. "I don't know. He's an evil, misguided psychopath. I doubt even his own mother could get him to stop."

"But…even evil, misguided psychopaths need a mother's love," Roark said with a wry smile.

Jackson nodded. "Thea, see what you can find on Francesca Martino. And while you're at it, examine Vincent's top capos again and get back to me with a full report. Oh, and keep me posted on the Secret Crush roses, too."

"Yes, sir," Thea said, heading upstairs. "I'm on it."

"What about us, Big Mac?" Roark asked, pivoting, Duff following him around.

"Stand watch," Jackson ordered. "Take shifts and don't dare blink."

"I don't ever blink," Marcus replied.

Eloise watched as they left. "I believe him."

"They're dedicated," Jackson said, turning to look her over. "But don't worry. You don't have to feel guilty about them, either. They love their jobs."

"I can't see how."

"They want to keep the world safe."

"Do you all think you're superheroes?"

"No," he said, his tone flat. "We just do our jobs and hope we make a difference."

She shrugged. "Let's change the subject. Are you hungry?"

"No," he said, his gaze moving over her face. "Let's sit down. I'm tired."

"Okay." She followed him to the sofa. "I wonder how Verdie's doing. She has to be wondering if I'm okay."

"I talked to her today," he said. "Sorry, that was the least of my concerns but she called *me*. She'd seen the news report. I told her you were safe and not to worry. And I told her not to talk to anyone from the police department or anybody else for that matter."

"So…no one's bothered her and Frank?"

"Not so far. I think she's in the clear."

His cell went off again. "Hello?"

"Jackson?"

Kristin's soft voice came through the line. He'd also called her earlier, afraid she'd hear an AP news report on the shoot-out and panic. "Hi," he said, getting up and turning away from Eloise. "Are you okay?"

"I just need to hear my mother's voice. Please?"

Jackson weighed the risks. Even though he'd called her, he'd told her to wait until she heard from him again. "It's not a good time."

"It might be the only time," she shot back. "I won't talk long."

Jackson turned to Eloise. Maybe Kristin was right. Things might not go as planned and then he'd regret refusing to let her speak to Eloise. "Okay. Keep it short."

He sat back down then offered Eloise the phone. "Someone wants to talk to you."

"Who is it?" she asked, clearly surprised that he'd let her speak to anyone over the phone even if it was a secure line.

"It's your daughter," he said. Then he handed her the phone and left her sitting there staring at it.

Eloise held the fancy gadget to her ear. "Hello?"

"It's…Kristin."

The voice seemed so near. Her daughter's voice. "Kristin." It wasn't a question. It was a statement full of awe and wonder. Tears hit like nettles against Eloise's eyes. "Kristin."

"I was worried," her daughter replied. "Just so worried."

"It's hard, honey," Eloise said. "It's always been hard. I…I did the only thing I could—to protect you."

"I understand that now. I never knew. I never knew you even existed."

Eloise thought about what the Veiled Lady had said to Jackson. Almost the same words. "I wanted to keep you safe. It was the only way." What if that was why Francesca had pretended to be dead and had stayed away—to keep her son safe?

"I don't blame you," Kristin said. "I just want to see you, get to know you."

They talked a few minutes more, mostly about Kristin's childhood. Eloise was glad to hear it had been a good one.

Jackson came back into the room then stood over her, signaling she needed to end the call.

It was too soon. A whole lifetime in a few minutes. "I…I have to go now," she said, her voice cracking. "Kristin, I hear you're getting married soon."

"I'm waiting for you, Mom. I want you there, please."

"I'll be there, baby. I promise. And, Kristin…I love you so much. Always remember that."

She heard the soft intake of a sob. "Okay. I love you, too. Bye, Mom."

The connection was gone, the phone quiet now. But oh, inside her heart, in that place that had ached and hurt for so very long, the warmth of hearing her daughter's voice brought a blossoming of hope to Eloise's soul.

She handed the phone back to Jackson then wiped her eyes. "She called me Mom."

"You're her mother."

His words were straightforward and solemn but his eyes held the faint sheen of moisture.

Eloise nodded, her hand going to her mouth as tears fell down her face. "I never dreamed…that I'd hear her voice again, that I could even hope to see her again. I never dreamed…Jackson."

He sat down beside her then tugged her into his arms. "Yeah, what are the odds, huh?"

Eloise knew the odds. And they didn't look very good from where she was sitting. But the man holding her made her feel secure and hopeful. Very hopeful, in spite of her dire worries and her fear that she'd lose both him and her daughter all over again.

"Let's go over everything once again," Jackson said. "From the top."

His agents didn't look thrilled about that demand. Maybe because it was nearly one in the morning. But his brother, Micah, had come up to Great Falls to meet with the task force and he didn't seem in any hurry to go to bed. "I'm willing to go over all the details again," he said.

"Brothers!" Roark shuffled the papers. "Can we do the short version, sir?"

Jackson stared him down. "No. I want the long and thorough version. Again."

"January," Roark began. "Special Agent Jackson McGraw gets a visit from a veiled female informant in his Chicago office. Informant tells him to expect activity from the Martino crime family soon. Old don is dying, young hotshot don is taking over and wants to 'avenge' his father." He went over the merging particulars of the case, from the time Kristin Perry had contacted Micah trying to find her mother and how in the middle of that, Micah had protected Jade Summers. "One capo arrested after trying to kill Marshal McGraw and Jade Summers but he's not talking. And in the meantime, FBI in conjunction with the U.S. Marshal's office discovers a possible leak within the ranks."

Jackson leaned forward. "Micah and I compared notes and realized these killings might be in connection with the Witness Protection Program and subject Eloise Hill, missing for twenty years." Here he glanced over to the big leather couch where Eloise lay sleeping under a chenille blanket. He'd insisted she stay downstairs until everyone went to bed. "Enter reporter Violet Kramer and Officer Clay West, who just happen to compare notes on the same subject and almost get killed trying to investigate." He broke down the details on that. "Veiled Lady informs FBI that Vincent Martino is still on the prowl and after Eloise Hill, who can't be located at this point. Leak keeps Mafia one step ahead of our investigation."

Marcus took over. "Hannah Williams, aka Jen Davis—also under protection regarding an unrelated case—hides out on ranch owned by Austin Taylor, nursing his ill daughter. Hannah threatened and almost killed—mistaken for Eloise Hill."

Thea pulled at her files. "Witness Protection subject Olivia Jensen reunited with her husband, Ford, after he tracks her to Montana. Ms. Jensen then set to testify against Vincent Martino in April, after witnessing him killing a man in Chicago. Olivia Jensen is pregnant and scared so her husband takes her into hiding to protect her. Mob locates them. Ford Jensen gets shot but Olivia Jensen does testify and Vincent Martino goes to jail, only to escape. Jensens now out of country under assumed names."

Jackson nodded. "Veiled Lady reports Vincent is out for blood and headed to Montana. Which brings us back to Kristin Perry, who visited Micah, talked with me here in Montana and in Chicago…and secretly attended the trial of Vincent Martino—where we believe she was identified by the Mob."

A gasp from the couch brought all of their heads up. Eloise shot up, her eyes wide. "My daughter was in Chicago at that trial?"

Jackson watched as she pushed at her mussed hair and got up off the couch to stare over at him. "Why would Kristin go to Vincent Martino's trial?"

"Excuse me," he said to the others. Then he got up and walked over to Eloise. "We didn't mean to wake you."

She pushed at him. "Do you actually think I was asleep? I've been lying there listening to all of this, wondering how in the world the Mob could keep killing women simply because they have green eyes like me. Am I so valuable to them that they'd try to kill anyone who attempted to investigate me or find me and that they'd kill my daughter just because she belongs to me?"

Before he could answer that, she rushed to the front door of the house and opened it wide. "Hey, I'm here. It's me, Eloise Hill, in the flesh. You want me? Come and get me!"

Jackson ran to grab her and pull her back inside, kicking the door shut, his hands on her arms. "Are you crazy?"

"Yes, I am," she said, shouting the words at him. "I'm on the verge of having a complete breakdown. I can't take this anymore. I can't."

He lifted his head just an inch, his gaze on their now-wide-awake audience. "Take a break."

The others scattered. But Micah kept his eyes on Jackson and Eloise. "You sure about this, Jackson?"

"Go," Jackson said. "Take five."

Eloise waited until Micah left the room. "I thought you'd told me everything. But you've been keeping things from me all along, haven't you?"

"I can't talk about all the aspects of this case, Ellie."

"But you should have told me everything regarding my daughter," she shot back. "Kristin shouldn't have gone to Chicago, ever."

"She came to see me," he said, wishing he could make her understand. "I didn't want her to attend the trial but she insisted. She wanted to see the man who was trying to kill you. And she wanted to learn more about his father."

"Well, I guess she learned a lot since Vincent has a hit on her now, too."

Jackson put his hand on her chin, lifting her head. "Ellie, you didn't need to know all of that. You only needed to know that you weren't safe. And that your daughter wants to see you again."

She looked distant, her anger coloring her eyes a dark green, but then her features softened. "I can't believe any of this. It's like a bad movie-of-the-week. All because of me, Jackson. Me. Tell me, did the Mob ever threaten Kristin? I mean, really come close the way they have with me?"

Jackson thought back on what he'd told her—only that Kristin had been and still could be in danger. Deciding to level with her, he said, "They came close once but she got away. After that, Zane helped to protect her until I finally convinced her to back off. Martino shifted gears after that and started concentrating on finding you. I think the leak probably tipped him off that the FBI was close to finding you, too, so he just waited until he could get more inside information."

"So he did and now, he's close." She leaned back against the door. "I'd rather he be after me than after Kristin." Then she lifted up, her chin jutting out. "I could be a decoy to lure him out."

"Absolutely not. No."

"But—"

"Don't mention that to me again, ever, Ellie."

She was about to protest when his cell went off. He held up a finger then turned to answer it.

"Agent McGraw?"

"Yes. Who is this?"

"Captain Lewis. Randall Parker just called me. He's going to turn himself in—just for questioning at this point, but it's a start."

"Are you sure?"

"Yes, sir. He said he's tired of running and he wants protection. The Mob is after him."

Jackson let out a long sigh. "Well, that is good news for us, at least. And, Captain, did you have time to go over that report my agent faxed you?"

"Sure did, sir. Looks like we have a case against Parker. We got a warrant about an hour ago to search his apartment and guess what we found in his closet?"

"The shoes he was wearing three years ago when he killed his first wife and put her in that hole?"

"Yep. The man apparently never throws anything away. And they are expensive shoes—in pretty good condition, too. We'll do a plaster cast of both prints to be sure, but I can almost guess they're gonna match perfectly. We gathered some other things from his apartment, too. We'll analyze the climbing rope to see if we find any trace fibers to match what your lab found. I'd say he won't be leaving after we get through questioning him."

"Thanks, Captain Lewis. Let me know when you have him in custody."

"Will do."

Jackson shut the phone then turned to Eloise. "Parker's giving up. He's turning himself in. And the captain's doing a comparison on the shoes we think Parker was wearing at both crime scenes and some other items they found at his apartment. He made a big mistake when he didn't get rid of those shoes."

Eloise sank against the door again. "Wow."

"The Mob's after him, apparently. He's going to jail to seek protection."

"Good luck with that," she retorted. "So one down and a whole Mob to go."

Jackson nodded. "Now at least we can concentrate on nailing Martino. Thea's already connected the roses to a farm in South America. We have agents in place down there and I'm thinking they're gonna find more growing on that remote farm than just pretty roses."

"Such as?"

"Opium—for heroin for distribution in the States. We've been trying to link to Martino through some of the drugs coming into Chicago. We might have enough evidence to shut their whole operation down once and for all."

She touched a finger to her scar. "That would be poetic justice, don't you think?"

"I'm not sure about how poetic it would be, but I'll settle for plain, old-fashioned FBI justice."

She nodded, her hand on his arm. "You should have told me everything, Jackson."

"I should have. But I didn't. Let's just get on with this so I won't have to keep any more secrets from you, okay?"

"All right." She stalked past him to the kitchen.

Jackson watched her then called out, "Hey, let's get back to work, people."

He heard a collective groan from the vicinity of the darkened sunporch.

FOURTEEN

"A quiet day." Roark turned from the window, the sound of thunder and lightning clashing out over the mountains.

"Not anymore," Marcus said. "Looks like that storm is finally going to let go."

Jackson rubbed a hand across the back of his neck. "We've accomplished a lot. Parker should be in custody by now and we've got some solid evidence on Martino. Even Parker could help there if he talks. He saw the two thugs at Eloise's apartment."

Roark stretched. "And we've matched hair fibers to both the rope we found at Ms Smith's apartment and the rope found in Parker's apartment—both containing fibers of his hair and Meredith Parker's hair. Yep, now if we can just find Martino, this will all be over."

Jackson got up, put his hands in the pockets of his jeans. "I'm thinking of taking Eloise out of Montana."

That got the attention of the other two men. "That might work, sir," Roark replied, "but what about Martino? He'll keep searching for her."

"Not if I get to him first."

"But…will she go for that?"

Jackson looked at Marcus. "Probably not, but we can't stay hidden away here forever. I have responsibilities back in Chicago. We all do."

Marcus let out a sigh. "Yeah, I so miss the city. Who needs fresh mountain air and all these trees?"

"We can keep tracking Martino," Jackson said, thinking this might be the only way to end things. "We have the lead on the Secret Crush roses and once the warrants are in place, our agents will be in on that."

"But that's a long shot," Marcus said. "The man has a whole slew of powerful lawyers."

"Well then, I'll keep digging," Jackson said, his voice rising. Outside, the thunder and lightning slashed across the sky in angry, rolling waves of black darkness warring with white-hot zigzags of light.

Both Roark and Marcus glanced at him and then at each other. "We're getting cabin fever," Marcus said. "Maybe we do need to try something new. What are you thinking?"

Jackson gazed up at him. "Let's go over this. We know Martino is close. Maybe we should split up, go out and scout around. Bring in the rest of the task force now that Micah's got Mac Sellers under wraps." They couldn't just sit here and twiddle their thumbs. "I'll put Micah on that. He and the two other agents *can* help us track Martino. We know his men are in the area but somehow they've managed to evade the locals and us."

He glanced toward the stairs. Eloise and Thea were up in their bedroom getting ready to turn in. "Of course,

Martino's power stretches to lots of places. He's probably got his own safe house around here somewhere. And he might have someone else besides Sellers on the inside."

Roark looked at Marcus. "I'm willing to go out and do a little recon and surveillance."

Jackson lifted his chin. "We've got a plan, then. I'll let Micah know to put the heat on and we'll do the same. If we have to turn over every rock between Great Falls and Snow Sky then that's what we'll do."

"That's the spirit," Marcus said.

Jackson shot the other two an appreciative look. He couldn't do this alone and thankfully, they were both a lot more objective about this case than he'd been. "Thanks, guys. We'll start first thing in the morning."

A loud clap of thunder silenced any further discussion.

Upstairs, Eloise and Thea were in their comfy sweats, both sitting up in bed reading by the light of the bedside table lamps. Duff was out on the landing in his favorite spot, right near the daybed where Jackson always slept.

"That storm sounds fierce," Thea said, her alert gaze moving around the room. "Maybe we should go back downstairs, ma'am."

Eloise looked at the clock. "It's getting late. I'd hate to wake everyone."

"Oh, I don't think they're asleep," Thea said, eyeing the door. "I don't like storms."

Eloise couldn't hide her surprise. "Theresa, you're one of the bravest women I've ever known and you're scared of bad weather?"

"I know it's silly," Thea said. "But my grandmamma lived in Kansas and we got caught in a tornado one time when I was staying with her. I didn't enjoy that."

"I'm sorry," Eloise said, getting up. "Of course we can go downstairs."

Thea was headed for the door when the electricity went out.

The house went dark. Jackson scanned the room. "Boys, everything okay?"

"I'll get a flashlight and check the circuit box," Roark said, already moving through the darkness. He came around the kitchen counter with a low-beam light. "I'll be right back."

Upstairs, Jackson heard what sounded like a door opening. "Thea?"

No answer. But he heard hurried footsteps, followed by Duff's whimpering. "Duff, come here, boy."

The dog yelped once and then went quiet.

Jackson felt it in his bones. Something had just gone wrong. Very wrong. "Marcus, upstairs!"

"I'm on it!" Marcus took off up the stairs.

Jackson grabbed his gun and did a quick scan of the downstairs, his eyes adjusting to the darkness. "Thea? Ellie? Everything all right? Marcus?"

Nothing. No answers and no barking dog.

He found his way up the stairs but couldn't see into the bedroom and he couldn't hear for the crashing thunder. But in a vivid flash of lightning, he saw Duff lying near the chair by the window. Hurrying to the dog, he immediately smelled chloroform.

He found Marcus lying just inside the door to Eloise's bedroom. His heart racing to beat the band, Jackson felt for a pulse and thankfully found one. Marcus groaned but didn't move.

"Eloise?" Jackson called. "Marcus, where are they?"

"Gone," Marcus managed to grunt out. "Hit me over the head. He took them."

Jackson stood up and looked around the room. The door to the upstairs deck was standing wide open, rain pouring in. And Eloise and Thea were nowhere in the room.

So this was it.

Eloise kept thinking that as she and Thea were being dragged through the pouring rain. Wet bushes and trees hit at her hair and face, but the man holding her didn't seem to mind the rain or the wet foliage.

Randall Parker had a gun to her head and his hand on her arm in a grip that showed exactly how angry he was.

She chanced a look behind. Another man had Thea.

"Bet you're surprised to see me, huh?" Parker said in a shout, his tone sarcastic and sure.

Eloise didn't want to talk to him but she had to know. "You turned yourself in."

"Yeah, I did. And then, my new friends got me out."

The Mob.

He didn't have to tell her the whole story. She knew how the Mob worked. They'd probably bribed a judge or paid a hefty bail or just hired a pricey lawyer to twist the truth. "They aren't your friends," she retorted, her teeth chattering in spite of the calm inside her heart.

"Better friends than anybody else around here," he shouted back. "Just shut up. You can save all your talking for Mr. Martino."

The calm didn't change. Eloise accepted that her life was about to end. She asked God to spare the others, please. Spare her daughter, the agents and Jackson, please. That prayer held her together and gave her courage.

"Where are you taking us?" she asked.

"You like the falls?" Parker asked, laughing. "Not the best night for a moonlight stroll but we don't have time to complain. Just keep walking."

He pushed her ahead of him. The rain tapered off to a steady drizzle. Eloise was cold and wet and to the point of no return, her cotton sweatshirt and pants clinging and heavy. Whatever happened from here on out, she had no control. And she almost welcomed the end. Heaven didn't have a Witness Protection Program. Heaven held so many possibilities to come out into the light.

Thea shoved into her. "Don't give up on me, ma'am."

Surprised that the young agent could read her thoughts, Eloise whispered, "I don't have any other choice."

Thea glanced back at the big man holding a gun to her head. "There's always another choice."

Eloise thought about that, the words washing over her like the rain. She remembered holding her gun toward the door the day Randall Parker had come looking for her. She'd had a choice that morning and Jackson had convinced her to make the right one.

Was she so willing to die tonight?

If it meant saving Jackson and her child, yes.

But what about life? The voice sounded loud and clear in her head. What about an opportunity to finally live, really live with the people she loved by her side?

The thought was sobering and exhilarating.

I do have a choice, she thought. *I do have a choice.* Then she asked God to help her make that choice. All along, she'd been praying to him to spare the ones she loved but what if *she* worked to that end and somehow managed to survive herself? Could she do that? Did she have the strength left for one final fight?

She looked back at Thea then turned toward her captor. "You're right, Thea. Thanks for helping me to remember that."

Roark met Jackson on the stairs. "Sir, somebody cut the power so the electricity and the alarm both went dead. The storm worked as a good cover."

Jackson heaved a breath. He had to remember to keep breathing, just keep breathing. "Did you see anyone?"

"No, but I found muddy footprints right by the circuit

box inside the open carport. "I came right back inside. Is everyone—"

"They took her. And they have Thea, too. Came in through the upstairs balcony. Marcus is down and Duff got hit with chloroform. I think they gave him a treat then put him under."

Roark let out a grunt. "What now, sir?"

"We track 'em," Jackson said, trying to focus on the work. And that meant tracking, staying alert, looking for signs. That meant not thinking past the obvious—finding the woman he'd come here to protect. The woman he loved.

He wouldn't think beyond that right now.

Eloise could hear the falls.

Parker pushed her toward the edge of a sloping rock where a square, covered pavilion stood as an overlook site. Down below, the water hit the rocks with a rapid fusion, running fast now that it had been fueled by the storm's rage.

A set of dim yellow lights glowed in the darkness, giving the little refuge a sinister feel. She could see the mist of rain in the light's casting glow.

Then she looked straight ahead to the man waiting there, a big bodyguard standing by his side. Vincent Martino looked sleek and elegant in his dark designer suit. He was comfortable and dry. And he was smiling.

"Eloise Hill," he said, his fat hands swinging wide, his dark eyes surrounded by sagging, puffy skin. "It's been a long time."

"Not long enough," Eloise replied, a new energy coursing through her system.

Vincent's smile died on his lips. "You don't understand, do you, lady? You don't see that justice has to be served."

"Oh, I see, all right," she said. "And I believe justice will prevail, in spite of all your efforts to stop it. You can get rid of me, but you won't be able to hide forever."

"Nothing worse than a smart broad," Vincent replied, his angry frown making his features craggy and ugly. He stared over at Randall Parker. "You brought me the woman. Now it's time to repay you for your service."

Parker smiled. "I'd appreciate that, Mr. Martino."

"So you want a one-way ticket out of town, huh?"

"Out of the country," Parker shot back. "Just like you promised."

"We can easily arrange that," Martino answered. Then he nodded toward the henchmen. "Push him over the side of this mountain."

Jackson's cell buzzed. Holding up a hand to Roark, he spoke in a whisper. "Yes?"

"Vincent has the woman," came the raspy voice. "He's going to kill her."

Jackson forgot the whisper. "Tell me something I don't know, lady. Tell me where they took her."

The Veiled Lady let out what sounded like a sob. "I'm watching them right now. They're near the falls— underneath one of those lookout shelters. It's to the west of your hideaway."

"You'd better be telling me the truth."

"I am, Agent McGraw. I'm going up there right now."

"No, don't—"

It was too late. The woman had cut the connection.

"No!" Eloise shouted the one word, watching in horror as the henchman came toward them.

Vincent started chuckling. "Don't worry, Ms. Hill. I'm not going to push you over with him. I've got better things in mind for you."

A chill grabbed at Eloise's backbone, causing her to bristle. Randall Parker let her go to stare at the man coming for him. "Hey, we had a deal. I find the woman and you get me out of here."

"That's what I'm going to do," Vincent replied.

"Not like this," Parker shouted. "Man, not like this."

"Did you kill your wife?" Vincent asked, his gaze locking on Randall Parker. "You'd better tell me the truth. My father had my mother killed, or so they say." He shrugged. "It happens, understand? But I don't like it. I don't like it one bit. Makes me sick to my stomach."

Parker looked doubtful. "It was an accident. We were arguing and she fell." He turned to Eloise. "I loved her."

"You pushed her," Eloise said. "And I want you to live to tell that to a judge."

"Enough of this reminiscing," Vincent said, a hand held up in the air. "I don't like talking about judges and

I really don't like wife-beaters. Get rid of the cop and the cute little agent. I'll take care of *Ellie Smith*."

Eloise couldn't let them kill Thea. She glanced back, hoping Thea would fight. The agent gave her a determined look, even while she was being shoved toward the stone-and-wood banister. "Thea?"

"I'll be okay, ma'am."

The agent sounded so sure. How did she know that? Then Eloise remembered all the agents wore those tiny transmission gadgets. And Thea always had her thin little cell phone in her pocket. Had Thea somehow managed to alert Jackson?

"Thea was smart to turn on her cell and send us a page," Roark whispered from their post about fifty yards from the pavilion.

"Thea's a smart woman," Jackson replied, his rifle scope centered on Randall Parker, because Randall Parker was holding Eloise. "They didn't take the time to frisk her, thankfully. Thea must have hit the GPS to alert us somehow."

"Let's go, then," Roark said, rising up.

"Not so quick."

"I can get a shot if we move a little closer," Roark replied. He tested the scope on the high-powered rifle. "I can take Martino out, even from here."

Jackson wasn't so sure. "What if you miss? They could kill both of them before we make it up there. And we need Martino alive so we can shut down his whole operation."

"Okay, then *what?*"

"Let's move in a little closer," Jackson advised, his own rifle solid in his hand. "We might have to take the quick shot but it's too risky from here. And they're too close to that ledge."

"You're the boss." Roark's tone told Jackson he wasn't so keen on this idea. But Jackson couldn't risk it. Not yet. Not when he could see Eloise and she was still alive.

But then, everything shifted as he watched in horror while one of the men tugged Thea and Parker toward the edge of the cliff. Jackson didn't have to think about things anymore. Tightening his grip on his rifle, he shouted. "Go, go! I'm right behind you."

Randall Parker grabbed Eloise and tugged her in front of him. "If I go, she goes with me."

"Oh, no," Vincent said. "That's not how it works."

Parker laughed then quickly whispered to Eloise. "Help me out here and I'll save both of us."

She didn't believe the man. He'd killed Meredith and he'd have no qualms about taking her down that cliff with him. She glanced at Thea. The agent stared across at her then tilted her head to one side, looking behind Eloise. What was she trying to say? Maybe that help was on the way?

Jackson, of course.

Eloise tried to stall. She glanced at Martino. "Why don't you let them both go? After all, you came here for me."

"Ah, such a noble gesture," Vincent replied. "But I

ain't buying it. They're eyewitnesses, honey. Can't have that."

Eloise shot Thea another glance. The man who'd dragged Thea up the slope had the agent against the banister now. Thea looked down at the cascading falls then back at Eloise. "It's going to be all right."

Eloise couldn't think about the falls. "You're right, Thea, because I'm not letting you go over this edge." Giving Thea a pointed stare, she used every ounce of her strength and elbowed Randall Parker in his midsection and followed that by a hard stomp on the top of his foot. He yelped and said something crude but her actions caused everyone to stop and stare. And gave Thea just enough time to squirm away from the ledge and take her captor by surprise with a poke of her fingers in his eyes. The man went down screaming while Thea grabbed his gun and turned it on him.

Vincent Martino shouted at the other guard. "Take care of this mess, right now!"

Then Eloise heard a voice booming through the night.

"Stop right there, Martino!"

Jackson's voice.

She whirled to see Roark and Jackson emerging through the trees with their rifles trained on Vincent Martino.

"It's over," Jackson shouted. "You hear me, Martino?"

"I hear you," Vincent said. Then in one swift move, he pulled out his own gun and started firing. A bullet burst through one of the weak yellow lights lining the pavilion, knocking it out.

Eloise screamed, watching the black shapes moving all around her. Thea shouted at Eloise to get down then took cover behind Martino's confused guard and tried to get off a shot. Martino fired back, hitting his own man. The other guard lunged to protect Martino and went down in a hail of bullets.

"Here, come over here!" Randall Parker stumbled up to grab at Eloise, pushing her to the ground and shielding her while bullets hit all around them. Then he toppled over, trapping her with his weight.

"No!" Eloise resisted, watching Jackson, screaming his name as she tried to claw out from under Parker's now-still weight. "Jackson!"

"I'm here, Ellie!" Jackson locked his eyes on Eloise then he grabbed his left arm and fell to the ground.

FIFTEEN

Eloise went silent, her scream locked inside her head, her heart cold with a solid, tightening dread. Randall Parker's dead weight suffocated her. A spot of blood pooled near her feet but she couldn't move.

Roark was still standing but so was Vincent Martino. They'd both managed to find cover. Both of the guards were down, one moaning and the other one staring up with lifeless eyes. She wasn't sure where Thea was. The mountainside had gone deadly quiet, the only sound the rushing of the falls down below.

Eloise forced a look to where Jackson lay. She wanted to call out to him but didn't dare. So she just stared at him, willing him to move. Just move.

He did, enough to lift his head and focus his gaze on her for a brief second. He was alive. Tears spilled down her face. Jackson was alive. She knew she had to do something, anything, to be able to get to him and help him. Eloise reached out a hand toward him. "Jackson?"

Vincent Martino whirled at the sound of her voice.

But Jackson was way ahead of him. She watched, horrified, as he let out a grunt of pain and rolled once, his rifle forgotten as he pulled out a hidden weapon and aimed it toward Vincent Martino. "Stop this right now, Martino," Jackson called, his voice raspy as he tried to stand. "We can end this here and now, you and me."

Vincent let out a bloodcurdling laugh that echoed down the mountain with a cackling cadence. "Sorry, can't do that." He started walking toward Jackson, his gun trained on Jackson's head. "I will gladly end it for you, though." He turned the gun toward Eloise. "By shooting her right in front of your eyes."

Jackson drew up, his own gun trained on Martino. "I don't think so. I'll shoot you before you pull the trigger."

Vincent pointed the gun between Eloise and Jackson. "Maybe I will just take out both of you and be done with it."

Jackson shook his head. "Think, Martino. Two other agents are with me. And they're both pretty good shots. You're surrounded."

"I don't care!" Vincent shouted. "I'm tired of this. I want that woman dead once and for all."

Eloise lay still, bracing herself, but then she saw a beam of light coming through the trees.

Vincent whirled, his gun hand moving erratically.

A voice called out, "Vincent, stop. Please stop!"

Vincent turned, shocked and surprised, his gun now on the woman standing just outside the tree line. "Who are you?"

Jackson stood, his breath coming in great waves. "Why don't you tell him?" he shouted to the woman dressed in black. "Tell Vincent who you are."

"I will. Just don't shoot him, please."

Jackson lifted a hand. "Stand down." But he kept his gun pointed on Martino.

Roark emerged from behind a jagged rock. Thea scooted around the dead bodyguard and hurried to Eloise. Tugging at Parker's dead weight, she pushed him over with a grunt and lifted Eloise away, helping her to stand. "Are you all right?"

Eloise nodded, intent on getting to Jackson. But Thea held her back. "No, ma'am. Stay out of the line of fire."

The woman slowly moved up the path then removed her hat and the dark scarf she wore underneath. "It's me, Vincent. I'm Francesca, your mother."

Vincent Martino let out a gasp and stumbled back. "No, no. My mother is dead. She's dead."

A man stepped up beside the woman. "No, she's not dead, Vincent. She's alive and she's here to help you."

"Ernest? Ernest Valenti?"

The capo bobbed his head, his beefy hand on the woman's arm. His other arm was in a white sling. "I'm sorry, Vincent, but I had to protect your mother."

Vincent stumbled toward the woman then grabbed her by the arms. "What are you saying? You've been alive all this time and you didn't let me know?"

Francesca nodded. "I couldn't contact you. He would have killed me. He almost did once. I tried to take you and leave and he had me followed. He took you away and ordered them to shoot me and throw me in Lake Michigan. But I survived, Vincent. Ernest was the one ordered to kill me but he shot me in the leg instead and then he whispered to me to save myself. I managed to swim to shore." She looked over to her companion then back to Vincent. "Ernest got shot in that raid the other day. He was watching over both of us. I did it for you, Vincent. I've been nearby watching, too, waiting for your father to die—"

Vincent's primal scream rang out over the trees like a screeching bird, its echo hitting the mountain. "Watching over me? Watching over me? You can't be serious. I thought you were dead!" He turned toward the man. "And you. I trusted you, kept you close by because my father considered you like a brother. And all this time!"

The big gray-haired man shrugged. "I love your mother. I've always loved her. More than I ever loved Sal. I've been hiding her and protecting her, waiting for the day he died. But I was always loyal to you."

"Not now—you've betrayed me." Vincent slapped the man then whirled back to the woman. "I hate you. I hate both of you!" Then he lifted his gun in the air toward the crying woman. "Things might have been so different, but not now!"

Eloise watched in horror as Ernest stepped forward just as Vincent pulled the trigger. Francesca cried out, grabbing at Ernest as he caught his stomach and fell to the ground.

Jackson and Roark both ran toward Vincent, tackling him before he could kill anyone else. "It's over now, Martino," Jackson said, bloodstains from his own wound covering his denim jacket. He looked back at Eloise. "It's finally over."

* * *

Eloise finished drying her hair and opened the bedroom door. Downstairs, she could hear Jackson going over the final details of the case. She walked to the banister to stare down at where they all sat at the big table. Roark, Thea, Marcus, Jackson with his left arm in a sling and his brother, Micah.

"Randall Parker is dead. But I think we can safely say that he killed both of his wives. We had a good case against the man."

"And justice was served," Roark retorted. Then he leaned forward. "I can't be sure, sir, but I think Parker threw himself in front of Ms. Hill."

Thea looked over at Roark. "He did. If he hadn't lunged for her and tossed her down, she might be—"

"Let's move on," Jackson interrupted, his head down as he stared at the files in front of him.

"Case closed," Marcus said with a hand up.

Jackson lifted an eyebrow then continued. "Vincent Martino is in custody and will be transported under heavy guard back to Illinois, where he will once again stand trial for murder, attempted murder, escaping from custody, bribery, drug trafficking and numerous other crimes. One of his top capos, one Ernest Valenti— who survived a gunshot from us and one from Vincent Martino—will turn State's witness and will be granted immunity and will be under protective custody until the trial is over and Martino is convicted. Francesca Martino will also be called to testify, but based on Valenti's statement and his willingness to testify against Martino, this should be the end of the Martino crime syndication." He stopped then sat back in his chair. "And I have it on good authority that Francesca visited her son in jail and had a long talk with him. Apparently, she asked him to turn his life around."

"From prison?" Thea looked doubtful.

"From prison, yes," Jackson replied. "He's still in shock from seeing his mother again, so he's pretty much tired and defeated. He knows he's been beaten, finally. I talked to the lawyer Francesca hired and I talked to Francesca herself. Vincent Martino has called off the hit on Eloise Hill, as of this morning. He gave his word to his mother that he won't bother Ms. Hill or her daughter, Kristin Perry, again."

"And you believe him?" Micah asked, giving his brother a hard stare.

"I believe Francesca," Jackson replied. "The woman can be very persuasive. And, like one of you said, even a psychopath needs a mother's love. And God's grace." Then he tapped the files. "Besides, we have it in writing and the man won't be out of prison for at least a century, if things go the way I think they will."

"So it's really over, for good," Roark said, flipping his ink pen in the air in celebration.

"For good," Jackson replied, looking up to where Eloise stood. Never taking his eyes off her, he said, "Eloise Hill, also known as Ellie Smith, is now free and clear and no longer under the need to have twenty-four-hour protection. Case closed."

"Not quite, sir," Marcus said, smiling up at Eloise.

"Clarify," Jackson retorted, still looking at Eloise.

"I think one of us will always keep Ms. Hill under twenty-four-hour protection. Just a hunch."

Jackson grinned at that and pushed up out of his chair. "Good hunch, GQ."

Then he bounded up the stairs to take her into his arms, Duff following him with a yelp of delight.

They ignored the laughter and applause from down below.

Eloise welcomed his embrace and his warm kiss. During the few days after the horrible scene on the side of the mountain, she'd thanked God over and over for sparing Jackson and her other protectors. And she'd thanked God for being The Protector.

Now, she drew back to touch a hand to Jackson's face. "Is it really over?"

"Completely," he replied, his gaze moving over her face with an open intensity.

She could see the relief in his eyes. He looked relaxed. And young again. She felt the same way inside.

But she had to be sure. "What makes you think Vincent Martino will keep that pledge?"

Jackson tugged at her hair. "His mother is counseling him. She's been visiting him as often as possible, bringing her Bible with her."

"And, just like that, the man's found religion?"

"No, not just like that. But Francesca tells me he's listening and he's asking questions. He has his mother back and…he has a certain obligation to honor his promise to her, as crazy as that sounds." He kissed her on the nose. "What are the odds, huh?"

Eloise laughed at that. "You might be right. I mean, here we are, together again. You kept your promise."

Touching his forehead to hers, Jackson said, "Almost. There is just one more obligation I intend to meet."

"Oh, and what's that?"

"I'm taking you to your daughter's wedding."

Eloise hugged him close. "I can't wait."

Then she heard a vehicle rumbling up the long road. "More agents, more files to go over? I thought we were all through."

"No more agents or case files," Jackson replied. Then he called out, "Thea, could you get the door, please."

"I'm on it, boss," Thea said with a wide grin. Duff barked and danced then ran downstairs to see what was going on.

Jackson turned to Eloise. "You have a visitor."

Eloise didn't have time to think. Jackson was tugging her down the stairs toward the big front door.

Thea opened it wide, then stood back, her eyes filling with tears.

Jackson pushed Eloise ahead of him. "Go on."

Eloise reached the bottom of the stairs and looked out at the steps.

And watched as a nice-looking man guided a young woman toward the open door. The woman looked up at Eloise and smiled.

"Mom?"

Eloise gasped, her hand going to her mouth. Clutching Jackson's jacket with the other hand, she cried out. "Kristin?"

"It's me, Mom. I'm here."

Eloise ran the rest of the way, holding out her arms to her daughter. "Kristin." Closing her eyes, she savored the sweet perfume of her daughter's hair, the feel of her child in her arms again and the warmth of the summer sun on her skin as tears of joy trailed down her face.

Finally, Kristin pulled back to stare up at her. "Now I can get married."

"Thank goodness," the man beside her said with a smile. Then he grinned at Eloise. "Hi, I'm Zane Black, your future son-in-law."

"Welcome to the family," Eloise replied.

Then she turned to Jackson and knew, at long last, she finally had a family.

EPILOGUE

September of that same year

"Nothing like a fall wedding, huh?"

Jackson looked over at his brother, hoping Micah wouldn't notice how nervous he was. Giving up on the crooked bow tie around his neck, he said, "I don't know. I've only been to a few weddings in my life, and most of those over the last couple of months." He held up his fingers, ticking them off one by one. "Jen and Austin got married in May, even before the case was solved—missed that one but I have a picture. Then, you and Jade, followed by Clay and Violet—married in August. And Ford and Olivia are expecting their baby—somewhere far away. Now Zane and Kristin, finally. It boggles the mind."

Micah slapped him on the back. "C'mon, you're an old pro at this by now. You got through my wedding."

Jackson lifted an eyebrow. "Yes, but I almost fainted when I had to give the toast at the reception."

"Jade thought you were so sweet," Micah replied in a shrill, girly voice. "She likes having you as a big brother." He turned serious. "And, in case I haven't told you, so do I."

Jackson pointed at Micah. "Don't go getting sappy on me. I might cry."

Micah pushed at Jackson's hand then fixed his brother's crooked bow tie. "You will cry, trust me. It's like nothing else, this falling in love stuff."

"I *am* in love," Jackson replied. "And I'm glad some of the others could be here today. It means a lot to Kristin and Ellie to meet these women—and their significant others, too."

Micah nodded. Off in the distance, they could hear musicians warming up out underneath the trees. Cellos and violins heralded in the celebration. "Too bad Ford and Olivia can't be here. But they send their best."

"I'm just glad they're safe and happy," Jackson said.

A knock on the door brought Micah around. "I'll get it."

Clay West and Zane Black stepped into the room. "Hey, y'all about ready?" Clay asked, slapping Jackson on the back. He looked over at Zane.

"I think we're all ready," Zane said through a grin. "I know I am."

"I've been ready for twenty-two years," Jackson replied.

Clay let out a chuckle. "Violet just finished the article, Jackson. The whole Martino story will be in tomorrow's Missoula paper. Including all the marriages and 'love-matches' that happened because of this case."

"She'll do us justice," Jackson said. "Violet is a great reporter."

"Justice, I like the sound of that," Clay replied. Then he smiled again. "But today, my friend, we celebrate. It isn't every day I get to be best man at such an unusual wedding."

Micah cleared his throat. "Make that—*two* best men."

Zane looked at his watch. "Let's get on with this."

"Anxious groom?" Micah asked, a teasing light in his eyes.

Zane looked at Jackson then mimicked Micah's words. "Make that—*two* anxious grooms."

In another room down the hall of the beautiful country church just outside Missoula, Eloise stood behind Kristin, both of them looking into the standing mirror. "Are you scared?" she asked her daughter, her hand touching on the delicate lace veil.

"No. How about you?"

"A little," Eloise admitted. "I've dreamed of this for so long, I'm afraid I'll wake up—"

"Alone and afraid again?" Kristin finished, understanding coloring her eyes.

"Yes." Eloise took a long breath. "But this is real, isn't it, baby?"

"Very real, Mom," Kristin replied as she smoothed Eloise's simple dress. "And it is a dream come true—I found a wonderful man and I found you, too. God is good, all the time."

"Yes, He is," Eloise said, hugging her daughter close,

the lace and satin of their gowns swishing around them. "Let's say a little prayer."

And so they did, thanking God for bringing them back together.

"And Thank You, dear Lord, for Jackson McGraw," Kristin finished, tears glistening in her eyes.

Eloise blinked back her own tears. "Now let's get out there before they both change their minds."

Kristin laughed, grabbed her flowers, then handed Eloise her own. "We're getting married."

"Together," Eloise exclaimed.

Jackson and Zane stood underneath the flower-encased open white arbor, plush yellow sunflowers growing all around them in the meadow behind the church. The prairie wind whistled along with the sweet sound of the music playing softly in the background. Jackson looked at Zane, gave him a thumps-up then turned as the wedding march began.

And then Jackson looked up the grassy aisle toward his bride, his breath hitching in his throat.

It had been Kristin's idea, this double wedding. But Jackson only had eyes for one woman. Ellie. His Ellie. She wore a cream-colored tea-length wedding dress. Not much lace, simple but beautiful, just like her. Instead of a veil, she wore flowers in her long brown hair and she carried one huge sunflower with a green ribbon tied around its thick, clipped stalk.

Kristin's dress was more frilly but pretty. Long and flowing with tiny little beads scattered across the full skirt. They both looked radiant.

Jackson's heart swelled to the bursting point. God was good. He could see that now. Ellie had changed him, softened him, brought him back to his faith. He'd already transferred from Chicago to an FBI field office here in Montana. He couldn't go back to Chicago. He wanted to be here near his brother and near Kristin, for Ellie's sake mostly, but for his own sanity, too.

He intended to keep Ellie in his sights, always.

And so he watched her walking up the aisle toward him, then he looked at the small crowd gathered to witness these two special marriages. His task force was here—Marcus all GQ in a gray suit and matching lighter gray silk shirt. Roark in jeans and a casual jacket, wearing a wildflower in his lapel. Thea in a pretty blue dress, smiling that Thea smile. And his brother, Micah, by his side, his new wife, Jade, beaming over at him.

Somehow, they'd all made it through and found new beginnings with each other. Somehow.

Eloise walked up to him, her smile radiant and sure. He took her hand, then waited with her as the minister performed vows for Kristin and Zane. Eloise cried and Jackson gritted his teeth to keep from doing the same.

Then at long last, it was his turn. He was about to marry his Ellie. He leaned close. "What are the odds, huh?"

She smiled up at him. "No odds, Jackson. Just God's love and grace. He let us find our way back to each other."

Jackson nodded. "And I will thank Him for the rest of my days."

She smiled again. "I'll be right there with you."

The minister cleared his throat. "If you two can manage to tear yourselves apart, we'll get you hitched so you can finish this conversation later, as husband and wife."

"I hear that," Roark shouted out from the audience.

Duff came running up the aisle, barking and dancing.

And so Special Agent Jackson McGraw took Eloise Hill to be his lawfully wedded wife, to have and to hold and to love and to cherish, forever. Then he kissed his bride.

While the crowd burst into laughter and applause, the echo of their joy floating out over the big sky and straight up into heaven.

* * * * *

Dear Reader,

This series was both a joy and a challenge for me. But being involved with the five other writers in this series was interesting and a great experience. I liked how we discussed the issues of writing such a dangerous and fast-paced series. We each worked to make sure things flowed smoothly. I hope you enjoyed reading the series.

I fell in love with Jackson McGraw when I read his backstory. He was a challenge as a character because I saw him as very hard-nosed and jaded. He'd lost faith in humanity because he'd lost the woman he loved. But Jackson saw a chance for redemption when he set out to save Eloise from the Mob. His love for her overshadowed every decision he made, but that love also held him together when things looked grim.

That's the way I see God's love for us. It overshadows the bad times and it holds us together during our trials. God's love never goes away. And just like Jackson, God fights for our love to the very end.

I hope this suspenseful series gave you a few hours of reading pleasure. It was my pleasure to write the final book and I truly enjoyed working with the other talented ladies who helped me tie up all the loose ends.

Until next time—may the angels watch over you. Always.

Lenora Worth

QUESTIONS FOR DISCUSSION

1. Jackson McGraw had a duty to his job. But he also felt he had a duty to protect Eloise. Have you ever let your personal feelings get in the way of your work?

2. How did Eloise's faith help her in this situation? Do you find yourself turning to God in times of doubt and grief?

3. Do you think Eloise did the right thing in asking Jackson to protect her child?

4. Jackson wanted to stop Vincent before he had any more women killed. Was that his only reason for going after the Mafia don?

5. Why did Eloise fight her feelings for Jackson so much? Do you think she was right to give up on their love all those years ago?

6. Jackson had some issues with this case that caused him to lose judgment. Do you think protecting Eloise clouded his focus in this case?

7. Why was it so important for Jackson to deliver on the promise he made to Kristin—that he would bring her mother to her wedding?

8. Have you ever made a promise that was difficult to keep? How did you deal with that as a Christian?

9. Eloise wanted to help her friend Meredith. Do you think she did the right thing, getting involved?

10. Should Eloise have gone to the police right away, after seeing Meredith's husband standing over her? What would you do in that situation?

11. Jackson and Micah had some brotherly tension to straighten out. Do you think this is common between brothers?

12. Why was Vincent such an evil man? Do you believe his mother truly helped him to begin to turn his life around? How?

13. The overriding theme of abandonment echoed throughout this series. Do you think Christians sometimes feel abandoned by God in difficult times? How can they overcome this?

14. Randall Parker did one noble thing before he died. Do you think this redeemed him even though he killed his wife? Why or why not?

15. Why did Eloise almost give up in the end? Have you ever felt as though you can't get past difficulties no matter how hard you try? How can being faithful help this?